Johann Wolfgang von Goethe

The Sorrows of Young Werther
The New Melusina Novelle

Johann Wolfgang von Goethe
Introduction by Victor Lange

HOLT, RINEHART AND WINSTON, INC.
New York/Chicago/San Francisco/Atlanta
Dallas/Montreal/Toronto/London/Sydney

Introduction

WHEN, in his later years, Goethe recalled the mood in which he wrote *The Sorrows of Young Werther*, he confessed to a feeling of surprise that so young a man should have achieved so explosive and radical a confession. He was not yet twenty-five when the novel was published in 1774. Apart from an historical play, *Goetz von Berlichingen, Werther* was his first major achievement. Its success was instantaneous and indeed so overwhelming that it would be difficult to think of many other works of European fiction which captured the imagination of their own generation with equal intensity. Its fame at the time rested, as Goethe himself somewhat uneasily recognized, not entirely upon its artistic merits: subtle and impressive though it was, its poetic qualities were not readily acknowledged. Much of its substance, many of its details were drawn from Goethe's own life, but it portrayed at the same time, with uncanny accuracy, the mood, at once exuberant and despairing, of a generation which had half-consciously turned against the manners and beliefs of the earlier eighteenth century.

Two years before the book was written, Goethe served as an apprentice lawyer at the Supreme Court in Wetzlar. There he met Charlotte Buff who expected soon to be married to Johann Christian Kestner, a dull but worthy official twelve years her senior. Goethe met her on June 9, 1772 under circumstances similar to those that brought Werther and Charlotte together; he found himself at once drawn to Charlotte and for a time attached himself to her, as much, it may be suspected, from a sense of frustration in the confined petty bourgeois world of the small town as from a feeling of profound passion. A few months later, on September 11, he parted from Charlotte and her fiancé on terms of genuine friendship. Shortly afterwards he received the news of the suicide of K. W. Jerusalem, one of his Wetzlar acquaintances, and this supplied the spectacular incident that was to lead to the writing of the novel. "As if in a trance," *Werther* was written in four weeks, "without a plan of the whole work or the treatment of any portion of it having previously been put to paper." Goethe used much of the correspondence between himself and Kestner (who had in the meantime married Lotte), and drew—especially for the second part—liberally from accounts which he had been given of the motives and circumstances of Jerusalem's death.

Such a combination of truth and fiction was, of course, part of a specific artistic intention: transcending his own personal role in the drama which he hoped to relate, he would convey with all immediacy possible the condition of a supremely sensitive, but supremely unstable human being. *Werther* was to represent the history, not only of an unhappy lover, but of a young man who is crushed and destroyed by the unbearable weight of his own passions. That this highly perceptive youth also found himself sadly, even tragically, in conflict with an insensible society, that he could not maintain himself in a world which persisted in its conventional social and emotional habits, must be regarded as a subsidiary though essential dramatic theme of the novel. No one knew better than the young Goethe how paralyzing such conflicts could be. In his life and in his poetry he had found no better way in which to show the extraordinary strength of his own youthful feeling and imagination than by a series of emphatic, even fanatical assertions of the creative freedom of the individual. Goethe's letters of that time, his dithyrambic poetry, and the enthusiastic passages in praise of Shakespeare's genius, are sufficient evidence of his rebellious faith.

But the stirring effect of the book was by no means due only to its social theme or the sentimental and emotional revelations of a private individual. As soon as the novel was published, it seemed to release, as Goethe himself later recognized, a latent disposition among his contemporaries to melancholy and crippling introspection. What was begun as the portrait of a gifted man of feeling turned into a tragedy of sensibility. Yet, Werther is no Hamlet, even though the paralysis of the will and the overtones of despair, of "sickness unto death" may seem to be shared by both: Werther, unlike Hamlet, seeks fellowship. Throughout his early days in the country he finds himself enchanted by images of the simple life which, in contrast to his disappointing experiences among society, he discovers in the world of Homer and the plain folk of the village. And what appeals to him in Charlotte is not the fire of her love for him, but the natural kindness of her whole being. His growing attachment to her, self-centered, demanding and naïve as it is, is hardly the kind of love which counts on reciprocity. It is rather an expression of his craving for a relationship which allows him to live wholly (if egotistically) out of the exuberance of his own emotions. Surely we must not conclude that he gradually surrendered to despair and thoughts of suicide because he realized that there was no hope of his marrying Charlotte.

The true reasons for the crisis in Werther's life and the cause of his collapse lie not ultimately in the circumstances of this unfulfilled love but in the incongruities of his own paradoxical nature. With an extravagant faith in the intensity of his feelings, he defies the society of his fellow men. As he realizes the hopelessness of his attempts at communication, he is compelled by a series of inner and outer circumstances to turn from the world. In his despair he dares altogether to deny its validity and relevance and eventually knows no other escape but to draw ever closer to the domain of nature, which is below man as well as above. More than once he declares himself outside the pale of what seems to him the meaningless and disgusting show of society, and by another short step he hopes to achieve a religious (or pseudo-religious) identification of man, nature and God.

There is yet another philosophical paradox in Werther. In the process of realizing his own exaggerated vision of human potentialities, he loses all confidence in the hopeful image of man such as the eighteenth century had created. He finds himself moved by the enviable figures of outcasts and lunatics who need no longer, as he sees it, to maintain the deceptive disguise of social pretenses. The idyllic and humane world of Homer soon gives way to the violent universe of Ossian. As the benevolently deistic God of the best of all possible worlds loses meaning for Werther, there emerges for him the terrible image of a nature-deity whose grand indifference to the petty concerns of man seems the only attitude of the godhead which the palpable imperfection of man's earthly career will reasonably permit.

In the experience of human insufficiency lies, ultimately, the key to Werther. The freedom of the human heart, which he so ardently declared at the beginning of his career and which he continued to assert with such uncompromising faith, is in the end used to accomplish the act of surrender, of voluntary submission to nonhuman, Godlike nature. In terms of this dilemma, Werther's suicide only completes the deliberate extinction of the last vestiges of the human personality. It is an act by which the freedom of man to recognize his own frailty and thus to deny the very meaning and validity of his life, is dramatically asserted.

Read in the light of such ideas, Werther becomes a work of extraordinary importance to our own time. We, too, readers of Joyce and Kafka, are profoundly moved by Werther's ever-repeated question after the essence of man. "What is the heart, what is the destiny of man?"—this is the memorable phrase which recurs throughout the book. Werther has no simple and no comforting answer to it. His jubilant faith in the passionate resources of the human being gives way to dejection and despair.

There is in Werther much of the cultural pessimism of his age and much of the temperamental impatience of Goethe's own youth. But it is not a document of academic interest only; its issues are universal: "The much talked about 'age of Werther,' " said Goethe in a famous conversation with Eckermann on January 2, 1824, "is not, strictly speaking, a mere historical event. It belongs to the life of every individual who must accommodate himself and his innate and instinctive sense of freedom to the irksome restrictions of an obsolescent world. Happiness unattained, ambition unfulfilled, desires unsatisfied are the defects not of any particular age, but of every individual human being. It would be a pity indeed if everyone had not once in his life known a period when it seemed to him as if *Werther* had been written especially for him."

If, then, we take *Werther*, not as a sentimental love story, but as the account of a complex psychological crisis, we shall all the more clearly recognize how deliberately Goethe conveyed its ramified theme.

It is not a "novel" in the sense which we attach to the great specimens of nineteenth century fiction: the area of its action is circumscribed and whatever "happens" in the slight story derives its importance almost solely from its significance for the psychological drama within Werther. None of the figures surrounding him, not even Charlotte, seem to have anything like the firmness of outline or the vitality of telling detail which are the essential ingredients in Fielding, Dickens and Balzac. As Werther loses his grasp of the world, as he longs in the true spirit of the romantic for immersion in the nonhuman universe, his own mastery of the world, whether in relation to others or to his skill in sketching, decreases and vanishes. "I have lost," he confesses in the letter of November 3, "the only joy of my life; that active, sacred power with which I created worlds around me, it is no more." It is at the point where for Werther all tangible reality collapses that Goethe carefully reinforces the narrative structure: he introduces the informed comments of the narrator and thereby gives substance and credibility to what might otherwise evaporate in the effusive monologues of the letters. With remarkable technical mastery, he weaves from beginning to end a distinct pattern of poetic motifs which mirror, as they recur, not only the passing seasons but the emotional attitudes of Werther himself.

Whatever literary examples may have been in Goethe's mind, they were carefully absorbed and transformed into a work of striking originality. Certain of its features: the epistolary form, the mixture of lyrical and melodramatic elements, the precision of psychological observation, the exactness of its pathological data, even, at times, the irony with which Goethe could not help contemplating the self-pitying utterances of Werther, are, of course, foreshadowed in the great writers of the earlier eighteenth century. Without the contemporary vogue of the melancholy poetry of James Thomson and Edward Young, without Rousseau, Richardson, Goldsmith and Sterne, the novel would not have struck its readers with equal force.

But its most enchanting quality lies in its lyrical prose which is incomparably fresh and musical and which has hardly been excelled by any other German poet. Still, it may console the American reader who cannot enjoy *Werther* in the original to know that Goethe himself at times preferred to read the novel in translation.

Werther was at once translated into several languages and, in Germany and elsewhere, became the prototype of a vast body of "Wertherian romances." Its effect upon the contemporary public was overwhelming and not seldom disastrous. Poetry was all too crudely transformed into reality, and countless suicides were ascribed to its abhorrent teachings: in Leipzig and Copenhagen its distribution had to be banned by law. Within a short time after the publication of the novel, a wave of "Werther-fever" had swept Europe. In 1784 a young English lady committed suicide and a copy of a translation of *Werther* was found under her pillow. In the announcement of her death this circumstance was particularly emphasized "in order, if possible, to defeat the evil tendencies of that pernicious work." One of the book's most distinguished readers was Napoleon, who carried it in his travelling library throughout his campaigns and who spoke to Goethe at their meeting in 1808 with uncommon critical understanding of the qualities and defects of the novel. Goethe himself was at first amused and later irritated at the spectacular impression which this most personal of his earlier books had created. In a brief prefatory poem to the second printing of *Werther* he concluded by urging his readers not to succumb to the fatal mood of the book. "Be a man," Werther's ghost exclaims in that poem, "nor seek to follow me."

In 1782 Goethe undertook the "delicate and dangerous task" of making a number of significant revisions for a forthcoming edition of his works. He toned down the exuberance of language, placed the figure of Albert in a somewhat more appealing light, and introduced the tragic story of the peasant lad, hoping thereby to throw Werther's own fate into clearer relief. Fifty years later he confessed to Eckermann in that conversation of 1824, that Werther is a creature "which, like the pelican, I fed with my own blood; there is so much of myself in it, so many of my own feelings and ideas, that I could have spread it into a novel of ten volumes." But with his characteristic fear of stirring up old wounds, he could later not often bring himself to reread the book. "It is a mass of explosives and I am uncomfortable when I look at it: I dread lest I should once more experience the pathological state in which I produced it."

Goethe was then no longer the restless youth; but even though he had in many respects changed profoundly, it would not be true to say that the issues of *Werther* had lost their significance for him. On the contrary, its substance, its nearly irreconcilable tension between the creative and irrational powers of the individual and the compulsion of the objective world, continued to be one of the main themes of his life's work. We need only remind ourselves of the anguish of *Tasso* or *Faust* as they face the conflict within them, of incomparable aspirations and the stubborn realities of the physical and social order. Goethe would not repudiate *Werther*, but as his life advanced, as his own responsibilities increased and his social philosophy matured, his conception of the function of the irrational underwent a remarkable transformation.

In the two great novels dealing with the education of Wilhelm Meister (*Apprenticeship* 1795-96; *Travels* 1821, 1829) and in *Elective Affinities* (1809) this change from the passionate romanticism of *Werther* to a more resolutely serene life becomes unmistakably clear. Quite deliberately he chose, later in his life, literary forms which should lend themselves to the communication of a more detached and explicitly ethical point of view. *Werther* was, not only in conception but in its style, the product of a lyrical and dramatic impulse. More and more Goethe turned later to the various possibilities of objective prose, especially to the reflective and, we may say, parabolical forms of the short narrative. From among the several dozen of these tales it is not difficult to justify the choice of the two here printed: they illustrate most successfully the turn in Goethe's thinking. And they provide, at the same time, splendid examples of his talents as a story-teller and prose artist. In some respects they are related to the eighteenth century tradition of the *contes moraux* and the philosophical and educational motives which produced them. But there is in them—particularly in the *Novelle*—enough of the characteristic admixture of the picturesque and the musical to remind us that Goethe, in spite of his dislike for the diffuseness and catholicity of the Romantic movement, nevertheless shared significantly in the climate of ideas of the early nineteenth century.

The title of *The New Melusina* (1817) alludes to the folk tale of the water sprite who had married Raymond of Poitiers on condition that he should never see her on a Saturday, on which day she reverted to her mermaid-like condition. He gave way to his curiosity and broke the compact, whereupon she disappeared. What attracted Goethe to this story, which had long been familiar to him, was not only the imaginative freedom of the fairy tale, and its formal flexibility but still more the ethical implications of it. It is one of three tales inserted in the second half of *Wilhelm Meister's Travels*, in which the force of passion overwhelms those who allow themselves to yield to it.

A loafing young fellow unexpectedly—and rather undeservedly—meets a beautiful woman; he is promised her love and her fortune if he will restrain his instability and impatience. Regardless of his good intentions he fails to keep his pledge; he is forgiven but fails again and is put to ever more severe tests. One day, he discovers, in spite of the girl's warnings not to be curious, that his beloved spends part of her time as a tiny dwarf. Torn between love and disillusionment, and threatened with final separation, he insists upon being once and for all united with his beloved, even though he is warned that this will inevitably reduce him to the dwarfish size of his wife. They marry but he soon regrets his hasty decision: he cannot forget that he is really a human being. "Now for the first time I grasped what philosophers mean by their ideals with which man is said to be so afflicted. I had an ideal of myself and often in dreams I appeared to myself as a giant." In the end he frees himself forcibly and regains human dimensions—poor and single as before.

Few other stories of Goethe's are told with as much humor and charm as this modern fairy tale, and nowhere else does he represent so vividly the restlessness of the human heart which, undisciplined and blind, reaches for the impossible, but which, reminded of its obligations, lends true dignity to man. By the excess of his passion and imagination the young man is transformed into a dwarf. But by the same dangerous energies that reduced him he is also, symbolically, restored to human proportions. If the "natural" and irrational, or, as Goethe would say, the *demonic* impulse is the cause of his degradation, it is also the source of his moral regeneration.

In the *Novelle* (1826-27) this central theme, not only of Goethe's but of all great art, is given profound and radiant poetic expression. We find ourselves, once more, in a world, which, like that of *Werther*, brings nature and man into the closest relationship and in which the high and the low, the naïve and the subtle, are gravely contrasted. But no one will mistake the nearly complete shift in perspective which now produces a masterpiece classical in its formal proportions as well as in its view of the stature of man. Those elaborate tableaux and the magnificent but circumscribed vistas to which Goethe devotes so much of the *Novelle*, point to a conception of nature which is essentially civilized: they are the appropriate background for the delicately sketched action and the muted harmonies that resolve it. They are, at the same time, the plausible setting for a highly formalized social hierarchy which, no matter how patriarchal it may seem to us, is here viewed as positively as it was deprecated in *Werther*. In this late work of Goethe's, man is able at last to cope with nature. But more than blunt force is required of him, and where he may believe to act most effectively, he will sometimes find his means ill-chosen and inadequate.

Honorio, though hardly the "hero" of the story, is nevertheless its central character. His love for the Princess, stated in the most elusive fashion, is the pivot of the action. He alone is always in sight, he connects the various strands of the plot, only he experiences something like a psychological change. It is true, that by his deed he averts an apparent danger; yet we are left in no doubt that, given the ever-present *element* of danger, his kind of action will not suffice—his heroism is soon shown to be foolish and useless in essence.

There is hardly a single incident in the *Novelle* in which we are not made to feel the presence of an elemental threat to the precarious balance of human thought, feeling and action. The individual, by himself or in his relations to others, must forever be prepared to meet this danger, and Honorio, brave, skillful, intelligent though he may be, has not yet recognized the essential duty of man: he has not yet mastered himself. The second part of the *Novelle* demonstrates in a symbolical and sometimes oblique manner the lesson which Honorio must learn. "You are looking towards evening" says the woman, perhaps suggesting the opportunities of America for the young courtier eager to prove his worth, "and you are right—there is much to do. Hurry, do not delay. You will conquer. But first of all conquer yourself!" This is the meaning which Goethe himself, in another talk with Eckermann, wished to stress: "to show how that which is unruly and untamable can often better be overcome by love and piety than by force." The tiger and the lion point to what Honorio must master in himself, and the child represents true victory and conquest. The story ends, not tragically like *Werther*, but on a note of conciliation and optimism: all tension is relieved, all fear banished by the courage and devotion of a simple heart.

Goethe's intention in relating this "extraordinary incident" cannot be questioned. But it may be objected that his proportions in the telling of it are altogether puzzling. The final unfolding of the main event is prepared with an overwhelming assembly of detail, and the narrative is frequently retarded by descriptive and argumentative passages of seemingly little bearing on the crucial action. Actually, however, a close reading will reveal it to be a work of infinitely careful organization. In 1797 Goethe had thought of using the plot for an epic poem, or a ballad, to be called *The Hunt;* the eventual title, *Novelle,* suggests a narrative in the style of Boccaccio or Cervantes; yet it is more in the nature of an anecdote than a short story, and it aims in the end at an allegorical and moral effect rather than at mere entertainment. "To find a simile for this story," said Goethe, "imagine a green plant, shooting up from its root, thrusting forth strong green leaves from its sturdy stem, and, at last ending in a flower. The flower is unexpected and startling, but it had to come—the whole green foliage exists only for the sake of that flower and would be worthless without it."

The style of the *Novelle* is disciplined and, while antinaturalistic, it is objective and rich in realistic detail. The emphasis upon visual and pictorial effects, upon shapes, outlines and deep colors, gives to it a wonderful solidity. From early morning, as the mist lifts on a brief, serene fall day, past the high light of noon, to the moment when the last rays of the sun illuminate Honorio and the child, we move in a frame of almost classic unity. At precisely the middle the story gathers speed: its sculptured, epic firmness turns into musical rhythm, and what began as a sober report of a hunting party, ends in a marvellous scene of transparent poetry. Beyond the last sounds of the flute there is no more to be said, no detail of fact to be added. What becomes of Honorio, of the company, of the lion? "All these things," Goethe assures us, "are foreseen, and therefore need not be said and elaborated. If they were, we should become prosaic. But an ideal, a lyrical conclusion was necessary; for after the pathos of the man's speech which is in itself poetic prose, still greater intensity is required and I was obliged to have recourse to lyrical poetry, even to a song."

If in some respects the *Novelle* reminds us of the architectural perfection of Poussin, its end, at once gay and profound, is pure Mozart. In theme and manner it is the superb achievement of the classical artist who renounces himself, controls his intensity and submits his instincts and his feelings to the ideal of self-mastery. "For what" conclude Goethe's own thoughts on the *Novelle,* "is the point of rendering reality? We are pleased when it is truthfully represented, it may even give us a clearer knowledge of certain things. But the proper gain to our higher nature lies in the perception of the ideal which comes from the heart of the poet."

Ithaca, New York   Victor Lange
January, 1949

Biographical and Bibliographical Note

JOHANN WOLFGANG VON GOETHE was born in Frankfurt in 1749 and, after a youth of brilliant creative exuberance, settled in 1775 in Weimar where he assumed a number of high administrative offices at the ducal court and where, at the same time, he devoted himself to a rich life of literary and scientific activities. The more than one hundred and thirty volumes of his works, letters and diaries reveal an incomparable variety of interests and accomplishments. He is, of course, best known for his dramatic poem *Faust,* of which the first part appeared in 1808 and the second after his death in 1832. But his lyrical productions as well, his plays (*Iphigenie,* 1787, *Tasso,* 1790), his poetic narrative *Hermann und Dorothea* (1797), his novels and his autobiographical, scientific and philosophical writings, all testify to a mind of rare maturity. When he died in 1832 he was recognized as the most conspicuous European man of letters of the age.

In 1855 the Englishman George Henry Lewes published the first comprehensive *Life of Goethe,* which is still a useful biography, in spite of obvious critical shortcomings. The most convenient summary of the data of Goethe's career, and a judicious bibliography is contained in J. R. Robertson's article on "Goethe" in the latest edition of the *Encyclopaedia Britannica.* Among more recent studies in English is Hume Brown's *Life of Goethe* (1920), J. R. Robertson's *Goethe* (1927), and two admirable books by Barker Fairley, *Goethe as revealed in his poetry* (1932) and *A Study of Goethe* (1947).

Nowhere, perhaps, does the personality of the older Goethe emerge more impressively than in J. P. Eckermann's *Conversations with Goethe* (1836, 1848) a document of splendid wisdom, comparable in kind to Boswell's *Life of Johnson*.

For the present volume the second version of *Werther* (1787) has been used and the translation of R. D. Boylan (1854) has been thoroughly revised and in many respects rewritten by the editor, who has also translated the *Novelle*. The translation of *The New Melusina* by Jean Starr Untermeyer is here printed by permission of Julian Messner.

V.L.

The Sorrows of
Young Werther

Whatever I have been able to discover of the story of poor Werther I have carefully gathered and here put it before you knowing that you will be grateful to me for it. You will not be able to withhold your admiration and love for his mind and character or your tears for his fate.

And you, good soul, who are filled with the same anguish as he, draw consolation from his sufferings and let this little book be your friend if fate or your own fault should not grant you one closer to your heart.

Book One

May 4, 1771

HOW glad I am to have got away! My dear friend, what a thing is the heart of man! To leave you, from whom I was inseparable, whom I love so much, and yet be happy! I know you will forgive me. Were not all my other attachments especially designed by fate to torment a heart like mine? Poor Leonore! And yet I was not to blame. Was it my fault, that, while the capricious charms of her sister afforded me agreeable entertainment, a passion for me developed in her poor heart? And yet—am I wholly blameless? Did I not encourage her emotions? Did I not find pleasure in those genuine expressions of Nature, which, though but little amusing in reality, so often made us laugh? Did I not—but oh! what is man, that he dares so to accuse himself? My dear friend, I promise you, I will change; I will no longer, as has ever been my habit, continue to ruminate on every petty annoyance which fortune may have in store for me; I will enjoy the present, and the past shall be for me the past. No doubt you are right, my best of friends, there would be far less suffering amongst mankind, if men—and God knows why they are so constituted—did not use their imaginations so assiduously in recalling the memory of past sorrow, instead of bearing an indifferent present.

Will you be so kind as to inform my mother that I shall look after her business to the best of my ability, and shall give her news about it soon. I have seen my aunt, and find that she is very far from being the disagreeable person our friends make her out to be. She is a lively, temperamental woman, with the best of hearts. I explained to her my mother's grievances with regard to that part of the legacy which has been withheld from her. She told me the reasons why she had done it, and the terms on which she would be willing to give up the whole, and to do more than we have asked. In short, I cannot write further upon this subject now; only tell my mother that all will be well. And in this trifling affair I have again found, my dear friend, that misunderstandings and neglect cause more mischief in the world than malice or wickedness. At any rate, these last two are much rarer.

For the rest, I am very well off here. Solitude in this terrestrial paradise is a wonderful balm to my mind, and the early spring cheers with all its warmth my often-shivering heart. Every tree, every bush is full of flowers; and one might wish himself transformed into a cockchafer, to float about in this ocean of fragrance, and find in it all the food one needs.

The town itself is disagreeable; but then, all around it, nature is inexpressibly beautiful. This induced the late Count M. to lay out a garden on one of the sloping hills which here intersect and form the most lovely valleys. The garden is simple; and it is easy to see as soon as one enters that the plan was not designed by a scientific gardener, but by a man who wished to give himself up here to the enjoyment of his own sensitive heart. Many a tear have I already shed to the memory of its departed master, in a summerhouse which is now reduced to ruins, but was his favorite resort, and now is mine. I shall soon be master of the garden. The gardener has become attached to me within the few days I have spent here, and, I am sure, it will not be to his disadvantage.

A wonderful serenity has taken possession of my entire soul, like these sweet spring mornings which I enjoy with all my heart. I am alone, and feel the enchantment of life in this spot, which was created for souls like mine. I am so happy, my dear friend, so absorbed in the exquisite sense of tranquil existence, that I neglect my art. I could not draw a single line at the present moment; and yet I feel that I was never a greater painter than I am now. When the lovely valley teems with mist around me, and the high sun strikes the impenetrable foliage of my trees, and but a few rays steal into the inner sanctuary, I lie in the tall grass by the trickling stream and notice a thousand familiar things: when I hear the humming of the little world among the stalks, and am near the countless indescribable forms of the worms and insects, then I feel the presence of the Almighty Who created us in His own image, and the breath of that universal love which sustains us, as we float in an eternity of bliss; and then, my friend, when the world grows dim before my eyes and earth and sky seem to dwell in my soul and absorb its power, like the form of a beloved—then I often think with longing, Oh, would I could express it, could impress upon paper all that is living so full and warm within me, that it might become the mirror of my soul, as my soul is the mirror of the infinite God! O my friend—but it will kill me—I shall perish under the splendor of these visions!

May 12

I know not whether some deceiving spirits haunt this spot, or whether it is the ardent, celestial fancy in my own heart which makes everything around me seem like paradise. In front of the house is a spring—a spring to which I am bound by a charm like Melusine and her sisters. Descending a gentle slope, you come to an arch, where, some twenty steps lower down, the clearest water gushes from the marble rock. The little wall which encloses it above, the tall trees which surround the spot, and the coolness of the place itself—everything imparts a pleasant but sublime impression. Not a day passes that I do not spend an hour there. The young girls come from the town to fetch water—the most innocent and necessary employment, but formerly the occupation of the daughters of kings. As I sit there, the old patriarchal idea comes to life again. I see them, our old ancestors, forming their friendships and plighting their troth at the well; and I feel how fountains and streams were guarded by kindly spirits. He who does not know these sensations has never enjoyed a cool rest at the side of a spring after the hard walk of a summer's day.

May 13

You ask if you should send my books. My dear friend, for the love of God, keep them away from me! I no longer want to be guided, animated. My heart is sufficiently excited. I want strains to lull me, and I find them abundantly in my Homer. How often do I still the burning fever of my blood;

4

you have never seen anything so unsteady, so restless, as my heart. But need I confess this to you, my dear friend, who have so often witnessed my sudden transitions from sorrow to joy, and from sweet melancholy to violent passions? I treat my heart like a sick child, and gratify its every fancy. Do not repeat this; there are people who would misunderstand it.

◆

The poor people hereabouts know me already, and love me, particularly the children. When at first I associated with them, and asked them in a friendly way about this and that, some thought that I wanted to ridicule them, and treated me quite rudely. I did not mind this; I only felt keenly what I had often noticed before. People of rank keep themselves coldly aloof from the common people, as though they feared to lose something by the contact; while shallow minds and bad jokers affect to descend to their level, only to make the poor people feel their impertinence all the more keenly.

I know very well that we are not all equal, nor can be so; but I am convinced that he who avoids the ordinary people in order to keep his respect, is as much to blame as a coward who hides himself from his enemy because he fears defeat.

The other day I went to the spring and found a young servant girl, who had set her pitcher on the lowest step, and looked round to see if one of her companions were near to place it on her head. I went down and looked at her. "Shall I help you?" said I. She blushed deeply. "Oh no, sir!" she exclaimed. "Come now! No ceremony!" I replied. She adjusted her headgear, and I helped her. She thanked me and walked up the steps.

5

I have made all sorts of acquaintances, but have as yet found no one I really like. I do not know what attraction I possess for people, so many of them like me, and attach themselves to me; and then I feel sorry when the road we go together takes us only a short distance. If you ask what the people here are like, I must answer, "Much the same as everywhere." The human race does not vary. Most people work the greater part of their time for a mere living; and the little freedom which remains to them so troubles them that they use every means of getting rid of it. Oh, the destiny of man!

But they are a good sort of people. If I occasionally forget myself, and take part in the innocent pleasures which are left to us humans and enjoy myself, for instance, with genuine freedom and sincerity, round a well-set table, or arrange a walk or a dance or suchlike, all this has a good effect upon me; only I must forget that there lie dormant within me so many other qualities which wither unused, and which I must carefully conceal. Ah! All this affects my spirits. And yet to be misunderstood is the fate of a man like me.

Alas, that the friend of my youth is gone! Alas, that I ever knew her! I might say to myself, "You are a fool to seek what is not to be found here below." But she was mine. I have felt that heart, that noble soul, in whose presence I seemed to be more than I really was, because I was all that I could be. God! Was there a single power in my soul that remained unused? In her presence did I not fully develop that intense feeling with which my heart embraces Nature? Was not our life together a perpetual interplay of the finest emotions, of the keenest wit, whose many shades, however extravagant, bore the stamp of genius? Alas! the few years by which she was my senior brought her to the grave before me. I shall never forget her, never forget her steady mind or her heavenly patience.

A few days ago I met a young man named V., a frank, open fellow, with most pleasing features. He has just left the university, does not think himself overwise, but yet believes that he knows more than other people. He has worked hard, as I can tell from many indications and, in short, is well informed. When he heard that I sketch a good deal, and that I know Greek (two unusual accomplishments for this part of the country), he came to see me and displayed his whole store of learning, from Batteux to Wood, from De Piles to Winckelmann: he assured me he had read all of the first part of Sulzer's "Theory" and possessed a manuscript of Heyne's on the study of antiquity. I let him talk.

I have become acquainted also with a very worthy fellow, the district judge, a straightforward and kindly man. I am told it is most delightful to see him in the midst of his children, of whom he has nine. They talk a good deal about his eldest daughter. He has invited me to visit him, and I will do so soon. He lives at one of the prince's hunting lodges, an hour and half walk from here, which he obtained leave to occupy after the loss of his wife, since it is too painful to him to live in town at his official residence.

I have also come across a few other curious fellows who are in every respect annoying and most intolerable in their demonstrations of friendship. Good-by. This letter will please you; it is quite factual.

------◆------

May 22

That the life of man is but a dream has been realized before; and I too am everywhere haunted by this feeling. When I consider the narrow limits within which our active and our contemplative faculties are confined; when I see how all our energies are directed at little more than providing for mere necessities, which again have no further end than to prolong our wretched existence; and then realize that all our satisfaction concerning certain subjects of investigation amounts to nothing more than passive resignation, in which we paint our prison walls with bright figures and brilliant prospects; all this, Wilhelm, makes me silent. I examine my own life and there find a world, but a world rather of imagination and dim desires, than of distinctness and living power. Everything swims before my senses, and I smile and dream my way through the world.

All learned teachers and doctors are agreed that children do not understand the cause of their desires; but no one likes to think that grown-ups too wander about this earth like children, not knowing whence they come or whither they go, influenced as little by fixed motives, but ruled like children by biscuits, sugarplums, and the rod—and yet I think it is so obvious!

I know what you will say in reply, and I am ready to admit it, that they are happiest who, like children, live for the day, amuse themselves with their dolls, dress and undress them, and eagerly watch the cupboard where Mother has locked up her sweets; and when at last they get what they want, eat it greedily and exclaim, "More!" These are certainly happy creatures; but I envy those others just as much who dignify their paltry employments, and sometimes even their passions, with high-sounding phrases, representing them to mankind as gigantic achievements performed for their welfare and glory. Happy the man who can be like this! But he who humbly realizes what all this means, who sees with what pleasure the cheerful citizen converts his little garden into a paradise, and how patiently even the unhappy people pursue their weary way under their burden, and how all alike wish to behold the light of the sun a little longer; yes, such a man is at peace, and creates his world out of his own soul—happy, because he is a human being. And then, however confined he may be, he still preserves in his bosom the sweet feeling of liberty, and knows that he can quit this prison whenever he likes.

◆

May 26

You know of old my way of settling down somewhere, of selecting a little place of my own in some pleasant spot, and of putting up in it. Here, too, I have discovered such a comfortable spot which delights me.

About an hour from the town is a place called Wahlheim.[1] It is interestingly situated on a hill; and by following one of the footpaths out of the village, you can have a view of the whole valley below you. A kindly woman keeps a small inn there, selling wine, beer, and coffee; and she is extremely cheerful and pleasant in spite of her age. The chief charm of this spot consists in two linden trees, spreading their enormous branches over the little green before the church, which is entirely surrounded by peasants' cottages, barns, and homesteads. I have seldom seen a place so intimate and comfortable; and often have my small table and chair brought out from the inn, and drink my coffee there, and read my Homer. Chance brought me to the spot one fine afternoon, and I found it perfectly deserted. Everybody was in the fields except a little boy about four years of age, who was sitting on the ground, and held between his feet a child about six months old; he pressed it to his breast with both arms, so that he formed a sort of armchair for him; and notwithstanding the liveliness which sparkled in his black eyes,

---

[1] The reader need not take the trouble to look for the place thus designated. We have found it necessary to change the names given in the original letters.

he remained perfectly still. The sight charmed me. I sat down upon a plow opposite them, and sketched with great delight this little picture of brotherly tenderness. I added the neighboring hedge, the barn door, and some broken cart wheels, just as they happened to stand; and after an hour I found that I had made a well-arranged and interesting drawing, without adding the slightest thing of my own. This confirmed me in my resolution of adhering in the future entirely to Nature. Nature alone is inexhaustible, and capable of forming the great master. Much may be alleged in favor of rules; about as much as may be said in favor of middle-class society: an artist modeled after them will never produce anything absolutely bad or in poor taste; just as a man who observes the laws of society and obeys decorum can never be a wholly unwelcome neighbor or a real villain: yet, say what you will of rules, they destroy the genuine feeling of Nature and its true expression. Do not tell me that I am "too severe, that rules only restrain and prune superfluous branches, etc." My good friend, I shall give you an analogy. It is like love. A warmhearted youth becomes strongly attached to a girl: he spends every hour of the day in her company, wears out his health, and lavishes his fortune to prove that he is wholly devoted to her. Along comes some Philistine, a man of position and respectability, and says to him: "My good young friend, to love is human; but you must love within human bounds. Divide your time: devote a portion to business, and give the hours of recreation to your sweetheart. Calculate your fortune; and of what you have left over, you may make her a present, only not too often—on her birthday, and such occasions, etc. etc." If he were to follow this advice, he might become a useful member of society, and I should advise every prince to give him a post; but it is all up with his love, and, if he be an artist, with his genius. O my friend! why is it that the torrent of genius so seldom bursts forth, so seldom rolls in full-flowing stream, overwhelming your astounded soul? Because, on either side of this stream sedate and respectable fellows have settled down; their arbors and tulip beds and cabbage fields would be destroyed; therefore in good time they have the sense to dig trenches and raise embankments in order to avert the impending danger.

I see that I have fallen into raptures, declamation, and parables, and have forgotten, in consequence to tell you what became of the meeting with the children. Absorbed in my artistic contemplations, which I described so inadequately in yesterday's letter, I had been sitting on the plow for two hours. Toward evening a young woman, with a basket on her arm, came towards the children, who had not moved all that time. She called out from a distance, "You are a very good boy, Philip!" She greeted me; I thanked her, rose, and went over to her, inquiring if she were the mother of those pretty children. "Yes," she said; and, giving the elder half a roll, she took the little one in her arms and kissed him with a mother's tenderness. "I left my baby in Philip's care," she said, "and went into the town with my eldest boy to buy some white bread, some sugar, and an earthen dish, for his cereal." I saw these various things in the basket, from which the cover had fallen. "I shall make some broth tonight for my little Hans (which was the name of the youngest): that wild fellow, the big one, broke my dish yesterday while he was scrambling with Philip for what was left of the food." I inquired about the eldest; and she had scarcely told me that he was chasing a couple of geese in the field, when he came running up and handed Philip a hazel switch. I talked a little longer with the woman, and found that she was the daughter of the schoolmaster, and that her husband was gone

11

on a journey into Switzerland after some money that had been left to him by a relative. "They tried to cheat him," she said, "and would not answer his letters; so he has gone there himself. I hope he has not had an accident; I have heard nothing of him since he went." I left the woman with regret, giving each of the children a penny and one too for the youngest, to buy some wheaten bread for his broth when she went to town next; and so we parted.

I tell you, my dear friend, when my thoughts are all upset, the sight of such a creature as this quiets my disturbed mind. She moves in a tranquil happiness within the confined circle of her existence; she makes the best of it from one day to the next; and when she sees the leaves fall, she has no other thought than that winter is approaching.

Since that time I have often gone out there. The children have become quite used to me; and each gets his bit of sugar when I drink my coffee; and in the evening they share my sour milk and bread and butter. They always get their pennies on Sundays, and if I do not get there after evening service, my landlady has orders to give it to them.

They are quite at home with me, tell me everything; and I am particularly delighted when I can watch their passions and the simple outbursts of their desires when some of the other village children are with them.

I had a great deal of trouble to satisfy the apprehensions of the mother, lest (as she says) "they should inconvenience the gentleman."

May 30

What I said the other day about painting is equally true of poetry. We must only know what is really excellent and dare express it; and that is saying a great deal in a few words. Today I watched a scene which, if I could only convey it, would make the most beautiful idyll in the world. But why talk of poetry and scenes and idylls? Can we never take pleasure in Nature without thinking of improving it?

If, after this introduction, you expect anything grand or magnificent, you will be sadly mistaken. It was only a peasant lad who aroused this interest. As usual, I shall tell my story badly; and you, as usual, will think me eccentric. It is again Wahlheim—always Wahlheim—that produces these wonderful things.

There was a coffee party going on outside the house under the linden trees. The people did not exactly please me; and, under one pretext or another, I lingered behind.

A peasant lad came from an adjoining house, and busied himself with the same plow which I had sketched the other day. I liked his manner; spoke to him, and inquired about his circumstances. We became acquainted, and as is my way with people of that sort, I was soon on fairly familiar terms with him. He told me that he was in the service of a widow and was fairly well off. He spoke so much of the woman, and praised her so, that I could soon see he was desperately in love with her. "She is no longer young," he said, "and was treated badly by her former husband; now she does not want to marry again." From his account it was so evident what beauty and charms she possessed for him, and how ardently he wished she would choose him to extinguish the memory of her first husband's faults, that I should have to repeat what he said word for word in order to describe the genuineness of the poor fellow's attachment, love, and devotion. It would require the gifts of a very great poet to convey the expression of his features, the harmony of his voice, and the fire of his eye. No, words cannot portray the tenderness of his every movement and his manner. Whatever I might say would only be clumsy. His fears lest I misunderstand his position with regard to the woman or question the propriety of her conduct touched me particularly. It simply cannot be conveyed, how charming it was when he spoke of her figure and body, which although without the graces of youth, had won and attached him to her. I can only recall it to myself. Never in my life have I seen or imagined such intense devotion, such ardent affections, in such purity. Do not blame me if I say that the mere recollection of this innocence and truth burns in my very soul; that this image of fidelity and tenderness haunts me everywhere; and that I consume myself in longing and desire, as though kindled by the flame.

I must try to see her as soon as I can; or perhaps it is better that I should see her through the eyes of her lover. When I actually see her, she might not appear as she now stands before me; and why should I spoil so sweet a picture?

June 16

Why do I not write to you? You who pretend to know so much, ask such a question! You should be able to guess that I am well—that is to say—in a word, I have made an acquaintance who has won my heart: I have—I don't know.

To give you a proper account of the manner in which I met the most enchanting of women will be a difficult task. I am happy and contented, and therefore not a very reliable reporter.

An angel! Nonsense! Everybody says that of the girl he loves; and yet I find it impossible to tell you how perfect she is, or why she is so perfect: enough—she has completely captivated me.

So much simplicity with so much intelligence—so kind, and yet so resolute—a mind so calm, and a life so active.

But all this is wretched stuff and mere pale abstraction, which tells you not one single concrete thing about her. Some other time—no, not some other time, now, this very instant, I will tell you all. Now or never. Well, between ourselves, since I began my letter, I have been three times on the point of putting down my pen, of saddling my horse, and riding out there. I swore this morning that I would not, and yet I am rushing to the window every few moments to see how high the sun is . . . .

I could not help it—I had to go out to her. I have just come back. Wilhelm; I shall have my supper and will write to you. What a delight it was to see her in the midst of those dear, happy children—her eight brothers and sisters!

But if I go on like this you will be no wiser at the end of my letter than you were at the beginning. Pay attention, then, and I will force myself to give you the details.

I wrote to you the other day that I had become acquainted with the district judge, and that he had invited me to visit him soon at his hermitage, or rather in his little kingdom. But I neglected to do so, and perhaps might never have gone, if chance had not discovered to me the treasure concealed in that retired spot. Some of our young people had arranged a ball in the country, at which I agreed to be present. I invited for the evening a pretty and agreeable, but rather dull sort of girl from the neighborhood; and it was agreed that I should hire a carriage and take my partner and her cousin. On the way we were to pick up Charlotte S. My companion told me, as we drove along through the park to the hunting lodge, that I should make the acquaintance of a very beautiful girl. "Take care," added the cousin, "that you do not lose your heart." "What do you mean?" said I. "Because she is already engaged to a very worthy man," she replied, "who is gone to settle his affairs upon the death of his father and to apply for a lucrative position." This information did not interest me much. When we arrived at the gate, the sun was about to set behind the hills. The air was sultry; and the ladies expressed their fears of an approaching storm, as masses of greyish clouds were gathering on the horizon. I relieved their fears by pretending to be weather-wise, although I myself had a feeling that our party might be interrupted.

I alighted; and a maid who came to the gate requested us to wait a moment—Mademoiselle Lottchen would be with us presently. I walked across the yard to the house, and when I had gone up a flight of steps in front and had opened the door, I saw before me the mast charming scene I have ever witnessed. Six children, from eleven to two years old, were running about the hall, and surrounding a lovely girl of medium height, dressed in a simple white frock with pink ribbons. She was holding a loaf of dark bread in her hand, and was cutting slices for the little ones all round, in proportion to their age and appetite. She performed her task in a most graceful and affectionate manner; each awaiting his turn with outstretched hands and happily shouting his thanks. Some of them ran away at once, to enjoy their supper, while others, of a gentler disposition, walked to the gate to see the strangers and to look at the carriage in which their Charlotte was to drive away. "Forgive me for giving you the trouble to come for me, and for keeping the ladies waiting: but dressing and making arrangements for the house while I am away had made me forget my children's supper; and they do not like to take it from anyone but me." I paid her some indifferent compliment; but my whole soul was absorbed by her air, her voice, her manner; and I had scarcely recovered from my surprise when she ran into her room to fetch her gloves and fan. The young ones threw inquiring glances at me from a distance; and I approached the youngest, a delicious little creature. He drew back; and Charlotte, entering at that moment, said, "Louis, shake hands with your cousin." The little fellow obeyed willingly; and I could not resist giving him a hearty kiss, notwithstanding his dirty little face. "Cousin?" I said to Charlotte, as I offered her my hand, "do you think I deserve the happiness of being related to you?" She replied, with a quick smile, "Oh! I have such a number of cousins that I should be sorry if you were the most undeserving of them." In taking leave, she impressed upon her next oldest sister, Sophie, a girl of about eleven, to take good care of the children, and to say good-by to Papa for her when he came home from his ride. She enjoined the little ones to obey their sister Sophie as they would herself, and some did promise that they would; but a little fair-haired girl, about six years old, said, "But Sophie is not you, Charlotte, and we like you best." The two eldest boys had climbed up behind the carriage; and, at my request, she permitted them to accompany us to the edge of the wood, if they promised to sit still and hold fast.

We were hardly seated, and the ladies had greeted one another, making the usual remarks upon each other's dress, especially their bonnets, and upon the company they expected to meet, when Charlotte stopped the carriage and made her brothers get down. They insisted upon kissing her hand once more; which the eldest did with all the delicacy of a youth of fifteen, but the other in a lighter and more impetuous manner. She asked them again to give her love to the children, and we drove off.

The cousin inquired whether Charlotte had finished the book she had sent her the other day. "No," said Charlotte; "I do not like it; you can have it again. And the one before that was not much better." I was surprised, upon asking the title, at her reply.[2] I found much character in everything she said: every word seemed to brighten her features with new

---

[2] We feel obliged to suppress this passage in the letter so as not to offend anyone; although no author need pay much attention to the opinion of one simple girl or that of an unbalanced young man.

charms, with new rays of intelligence, which appeared to increase gradually, as she felt that I understood her.

"When I was younger," she said, "I loved nothing so much as novels. Nothing could equal my delight when, on Sundays, I could settle down quietly in a corner and enter with my whole heart and soul into the joys or sorrows of some Miss Jenny. I do not deny that they possess some charms for me yet. But I read so seldom that I prefer books that suit my taste. And I like those authors best who describe my own situation in life—and the friends who are about me— whose stories touch me with interest because they resemble my own domestic life, which is perhaps not absolutely paradise, but on the whole a source of indescribable happiness."

I tried to conceal the emotion which these words aroused, but it was of slight avail; for when she incidentally expressed her opinion of "The Vicar of Wakefield," and of other works,[3] I could no longer contain myself but said what I thought of it; and it was not until Charlotte had addressed herself to the other two ladies that I remembered their presence, and observed them sitting silent and astonished. The cousin looked at me several times with a mocking air, which, however, I did not at all mind.

We talked of the pleasures of dancing. "If it is a fault to love it," said Charlotte, "I confess that I prize it above all other amusements. If anything worries me, I go to my old squeaky piano, drum out a quadrille, and everything is well again."

How I gazed into her rich dark eyes as she spoke; how my own eyes hung on her warm lips and fresh, glowing cheeks, how I became lost in the delightful sound of what she said —so much so, that I often did not hear her actual words. In short, when we arrived at the dance, I alighted from the carriage

[3] Though the names of some of our native authors are omitted, whoever shares Charlotte's approbation will feel in his heart who they are, if he should read this passage. And no one else needs to know.

as if in a dream, and was so lost in the dim world around me that I scarcely heard the music which came from the brightly lit ballroom.

Two gentlemen, Mr. Audran and a certain N. N. (I cannot be bothered with names), who were the cousin's and Charlotte's partners, received us at the carriage door, and took charge of their ladies while I followed with mine.

We danced a minuet. I engaged one lady after another, and it seemed to me that precisely the most disagreeable could not bring themselves to change partners and end the figure. Charlotte and her partner began an English quadrille, and you must imagine my delight when it was her turn to dance the figure with us. You should see Charlotte dance. She dances with her whole heart and soul: her body is all harmony, elegance, and grace, as if nothing else mattered, as if she had no other thought or feeling; and, doubtless, for the moment, everything else has ceased to exist for her.

She was engaged for the second quadrille, but promised me the third, and assured me, with the most disarming ingenuousness, that she was very fond of the German way of dancing. "It is the custom here," she said, "for the previous partners to dance the German dance together; but my partner is an indifferent waltzer, and will feel delighted if I save him the trouble. Your partner cannot waltz, and does not like it either: but I noticed during the quadrille that you waltz well; so, if you will waltz with me, do propose it to my partner, and I will ask yours." We agreed, and it was arranged that while we danced our partners should entertain each other.

We began, and at first delighted ourselves with the usual graceful motions of the arms. With what charm, what ease she moved! When the waltz started, and the dancers whirled round each other like planets in the sky, there was some confusion, since some of the dancers were fairly clumsy. We kept back, allowing the others to wear themselves out; and when the most awkward dancers had left the floor, we joined in and kept it up with one other couple—Audran and his partner. Never had I danced more lightly. I felt myself more than mortal, holding this loveliest of creatures in my arms, flying with her like the wind, till I lost sight of everything else; and—Wilhelm, I vowed at that moment that a girl whom I loved, or for whom I felt the slightest attachment, should never waltz with another, even if it should be my end! You will understand.

We took a few turns in the room to recover our breath. Then Charlotte sat down and ate some oranges that I had secured —the only ones left; but at every slice which she politely offered to a greedy lady sitting next to her, I felt as though a dagger went through my heart.

We were the second couple in the third quadrille. As we were dancing along (and Heaven knows with what ecstasy I gazed at her eyes which shone with the sweetest feeling of enjoyment), we passed a lady whom I had noticed because of her charming expression, although she was no longer young. She looked at Charlotte with a smile, shook her finger at her, and repeated twice significantly the name Albert.

"Who is Albert," I asked Charlotte, "if it is not impertinent?" She was about to answer, when we had to separate, in order to execute the figure of eight; and as we crossed in front of each other, I noticed that she looked somewhat pensive. "Why should I conceal it from you?" she said, as she gave me her hand for the promenade. "Albert is a worthy man, to whom I am as good as engaged." Now, there was nothing new to me in this (the girls had told me of it on the way); yet it struck me as new since I had not thought of it in connection with her whom in so short a time I had grown to like so much. At any rate, I became confused, got out of the figure, and caused general confusion; so that it took Charlotte's whole presence of mind to straighten me out by pulling and pushing me into my proper place.

The dance was not yet finished when the lightning which we had for some time seen on the horizon and which I had pretended was only summer lightning, grew more violent; and the thunder was heard above the music. When any distress or terror interrupts our amusements, it naturally makes a deeper impression than at other times, partly because the contrast makes us more keenly susceptible, or rather perhaps because our senses are then more open to impressions, and the shock is consequently stronger. To this cause I must ascribe the looks of fear on the faces of the ladies. One wisely sat down in a corner with her back to the window, and held her hands over her ears; a second knelt down and hid her face in the other's lap; a third pushed herself between them, and embraced her sisters with a thousand tears; some insisted on going home; others, unaware of what they were doing, lacked sufficient presence of mind to avoid the impertinences of their partners, who had had something to drink and who sought to capture for themselves those sighs which the lips of our distressed beauties had intended for Heaven. Some of the gentlemen had gone downstairs to smoke a quiet pipe, and the rest of the company gladly accepted a happy suggestion of the hostess to retire into another room which had shutters and curtains. We had hardly got there when Charlotte arranged the chairs in a circle; and when the company had sat down at her request, she proposed a game.

I noticed some of the guests purse their lips and stretch themselves at the prospect of some agreeable forfeit. "Let us play at counting," said Charlotte. "Now, pay attention: I shall go round the circle from right to left; and each one is to count one after the other, the number that comes to him, but he must count fast; whoever hesitates or makes a mistake gets a box on the ear, and so on, till we have counted a thousand." It was delightful to see the fun. She went round the circle with up-raised arm. "One," said the first; "two," the second; "three," the third; and so on, till Charlotte went faster and faster. One man made a mistake—instantly a box on the ear; and amid the laughter that ensued, another box; and so on, faster and faster.

I myself came in for two. I imagined that they were harder than the rest, but felt quite delighted. General laughter and commotion put an end to the game long before we had counted to a thousand. The party broke up into little separate groups; the storm was over, and I followed Charlotte into the ballroom. On the way she said, "The boxes on the ear made them forget their fears of the storm." I could make no reply. "I," she continued, "was as much frightened as any of them; but by pretending to be brave, to keep up the spirits of the others, I forgot my own fears." We went to the window. It was still thundering in the distance; a soft rain was pouring down over the country, and filled the air around us with delicious fragrance. Charlotte leaned on her elbow; her eyes wandered over the scene; she looked up to the sky, and then turned to me; her eyes were filled with tears; she put her hand on mine and said, "Klopstock!" I remembered at once that magnificent ode of his which was in her thoughts, and felt overcome by the flood of emotion which the mention of his name called forth. It was more than I could bear. I bent over her hand, kissed it in a stream of ecstatic tears, and again looked into her eyes. Divine Klopstock! If only you could have seen your apotheosis in those eyes! And your name, so often profaned, would that I never heard it repeated!

———————◆———————

June 19

I no longer remember where I stopped in my story. I only know that it was two in the morning when I went to bed; and if you had been with me and I might have talked instead of writing to you, I should probably have kept you up till daylight.

I think I have not yet told you what happened as we rode

home from the ball, nor have I time to tell you now. It was a magnificent sunrise; the whole country was fresh, and the dew fell drop by drop from the trees. Our companions were nodding. Charlotte asked me if I did not want to join them, and urged me not to stand on ceremony. Looking at her, I answered, "As long as I see those eyes open, there is no danger of my falling asleep." We both kept awake till we reached her gate. The maid opened it quietly and assured her, in answer to her inquiries, that her father and the children were well, and still sleeping. I left, asking my permission to see her that day. She consented, and I kept my promise; and since that time sun, moon, and stars may pursue their course: I know not whether it is day or night; the whole world about me has ceased to be.

———◆———

June 21

My days are as happy as those God gives to his saints; and whatever be my fate hereafter, I can never say that I have not tasted joy—the purest joys of life. You know my Wahlheim. I am now completely settled there. It is only half an hour from Charlotte: and there I feel that I am myself, and taste all the happiness which can fall to the lot of man.

Little did I imagine, when I selected Wahlheim as the goal of my walks, that all Heaven lay so near it. How often, in my wanderings from the hillside or from the meadows across the river had I seen this hunting lodge, which now holds all the joys of my heart!

I have often reflected, dear Wilhelm, on the eagerness of men to wander about and make new discoveries, and on that secret urge which afterwards makes them return to their narrow circle, conform to the customary path, and pay no attention to the right or the left.

It is so strange how, when I came here first and looked out upon that lovely valley from the hills, I felt charmed with everything around me—the little wood opposite—how delightful to sit in its shade! How fine the view from that summit!—that delightful chain of hills, and the exquisite valleys at their feet!—could I but lose myself amongst them!—I hurried, and returned without finding what I sought. Distance, my friend, is like the future. A dim vastness is spread before our souls; our feelings are as obscure as our vision, and we desire to surrender our whole being, that it may be filled with the perfect bliss of one glorious emotion—but alas! when we rush towards our goal, when the distant *there* becomes the present *here*, all is the same; we are as poor and circumscribed as ever, and our soul still languishes for unattainable happiness.

So does the restless traveler long at last for his native soil, and finds in his own cottage, in the arms of his wife, in the affection of his children, and the labor necessary for their support, all that happiness which he sought in vain in the wide world.

When I go out to Wahlheim at sunrise, and with my own hands gather in the garden the sugar peas for my own dinner; and when I sit down to string them as I read my Homer, and then, selecting a saucepan from the little kitchen, fetch my own butter, put my peas on the fire, cover the pot, and sit down to stir it occasionally—I vividly recall the illustrious suitors of Penelope, killing, dressing, and roasting their own oxen and swine. Nothing fills me with a more pure and genuine happiness than those traits of patriarchal life which, thank Heaven! I can imitate without affectation. Happy I am that my heart can feel the same simple and innocent pleasure as the peasant whose table is covered with food of his own growing, and who not only enjoys his meal, but remembers with delight the happy days, and the sunny morning when he planted it, the mild evenings when he watered it, and the pleasure he experienced in watching its daily growth.

The day before yesterday the physician came from the town to pay a visit to the judge. He found me on the floor playing with Charlotte's brothers and sisters. Some of them were scrambling over me, and others romped with me; and as I caught and tickled them, they made a great uproar. The doctor is the sort of person who adjusts his stuffy cuffs, and continually settles his frill while he is talking; he thought my conduct beneath the dignity of a sensible man. I could see it in his face; but I did not let myself be disturbed, and allowed him to continue his wise talk, while I rebuilt the children's card houses as fast as they threw them down. He went about the town afterwards, complaining that the judge's children were spoiled enough, but that now Werther was completely ruining them.

Yes, Wilhelm, nothing on this earth is closer to my heart than children. When I watch their doings; when I see in the little creatures the seeds of all those virtues and qualities, which they will one day find so indispensable; when I see in their obstinacy all the future firmness and constancy of a noble character, in their capriciousness that gaiety of temper which will carry them over the dangers and troubles of life so simple and unspoiled, I always remember the golden words of the Great Teacher of mankind, "Unless ye become even as one of these." And yet, my friend, these children, who are our equals, whom we ought to consider models—we treat them as though they were our inferiors. They are supposed to have no will of their own! And have we none ourselves? Whence our superiority? Is it because we are older and more experienced? Great God! from the height of Thy Heaven Thou beholdest great children and little children, and no others; and Thy Son has long since declared which afford Thee greater pleasure. But they will not believe in Him, and hear Him not—that, too, is an old story; and they train their children after their own image, and—

Adieu, Wilhelm, I must not continue this useless talk.

———————◆———————

What Charlotte can be to an invalid I feel in my own heart, which suffers more than many a poor creature lingering on a bed of sickness. She will spend a few days in the town with a woman, whom the physicians have almost given up, and who wishes to have Charlotte near her in her last moments. I accompanied her last week on a visit to the vicar of St., a village in the mountains, about an hour away. We arrived about four o'clock. Charlotte had taken her little sister with her. When we entered the courtyard of the vicarage, we found the good old man sitting on a bench before the door, in the shade of two large walnut trees. At the sight of Charlotte, he seemed to gain fresh life, rose, forgot his knotty stick, and ventured to walk towards her. She ran to him, and made him sit down; then, placing herself by his side, she gave him her father's greetings, and then caught up his youngest child—a dirty, ugly little thing, but the joy of his old age. I wish you could have seen her attention to this old man—how she raised her voice because of his deafness; how she told him of perfectly healthy young people who had died when it was least expected; praised the virtues of Karlsbad, and commended his decision to spend the next summer there; and assured him that he looked better and stronger than when she saw him last. I, in the meantime, paid my respects to his good wife. The old man seemed in excellent spirits; and, as I could not help admiring the beauty of the walnut trees, which formed such an agreeable shade over us, he began, though with some little difficulty, to tell us their history. "The older," he said, "we do not know who planted it—some say one vicar, and some say another; but the younger one, there behind us, is exactly the age of my wife—fifty years next October. Her father planted it the morning of the day she was born. My wife's father was my predecessor here, and I cannot tell you how fond he was of that tree; and it is quite as dear to me. Under the shade of that very tree, on a log, my wife was seated, knitting, when I came into this courtyard for the first time as a poor student, just seven and twenty years ago." Charlotte inquired after his daughter. He said she had gone with Mr. Schmidt to the workers in the field. The old man then resumed his story, and told us how his predecessor had taken a fancy to him, as had his daughter; and how he had become first his curate, and subsequently his successor. He had scarcely finished his story when his daughter returned through the garden, accompanied by Mr. Schmidt. She welcomed Charlotte affectionately, and I confess I was much taken with her appearance. She was a lively looking, good-humored brunette, good company for a short stay in the country. Her suitor (for such Mr. Schmidt appeared to be) was a polite but reserved person who would not join our conversation, in spite of Charlotte's efforts to draw him out. I was much annoyed to see by his expression that his silence was not due to any dullness or stupidity, but to caprice and ill-humor. This became only too evident when we set out to take a walk, and Friederike went along with Charlotte. The worthy gentleman's face, which was naturally rather somber, became so dark and angry that Charlotte had to touch my arm and remind me that I was talking too much to Friederike. Nothing distresses me more than to see people torment each other; particularly when young people, in the very season of pleasure, waste their few short days of sunshine in quarrels and trifles, and only perceive their error when it is too late. This thought preoccupied me; and in the evening, when we returned to the vicar's, and were sitting round the table with our bread and milk, the conversation turned on the joys and sorrows of the world, and I could not resist the temptation to attack bitterly ill-humor. "We are apt," I began, "to complain, but surely with very little reason, that our happy days are few, and our days of sorrow are many. If our hearts were always disposed to receive what God sends us every day, we should have strength enough to bear misery when it comes." "But," observed the vicar's wife, "we cannot always control our tempers, so much depends upon our nature; when the body suffers, the mind is ill at ease." "I admit that," I continued, "but let us regard it as a disease, and ask whether there is no remedy for it." "That sounds plausible," said Charlotte, "at least, I think, very much depends upon ourselves; I know it is so with me. When anything annoys and disturbs me, I run into the garden, hum a couple of dance tunes, and everything is all right again." "That is what I meant," I replied. "Ill-humor resembles laziness: it is natural to us; but if once we have courage to exert ourselves, our work runs fresh from our hands, and we find real enjoyment in doing." Friederike listened very attentively; and the young man objected that we are not masters of ourselves, and still less so of our feelings. "We are talking about a disagreeable emotion," I added, "from which everyone would gladly escape, but none know their own powers without trial. Surely sick people are glad to consult doctors, and submit to the most scrupulous regimen, the most nauseous medicines, in order to recover their health." I noticed that the good old man inclined his head, and strained to hear our discourse. I raised my voice and addressed myself directly to him. "They preach against a great many vices," I observed, "but I can't remember a sermon against ill-humor."[4] "That should be done by your town clergymen," he replied; "country people are never ill-humored; still, it might be useful occasionally—to our

---

[4] We have an excellent sermon on this subject by Lavater, among those on the Book of Jonas.

wives, for instance, and the judge." We all laughed, and he joined us so vigorously that he was seized by a fit of coughing, which interrupted our conversation for a time. Mr. Schmidt resumed the subject. "You call ill-humor a vice," he remarked, "but I think you exaggerate." "Not at all," I replied, "if that deserves the name which is pernicious to ourselves and our neighbors. Is it not enough that we lack the power to make one another happy, must we deprive each other of the pleasure which each of us can at times feel in his heart? Show me the man who has the courage to hide his ill-humor, who bears the whole burden himself without disturbing the happiness of those around him. No; ill-humor arises from a sense of our own inadequacy—from a discontent with ourselves and an hostility towards others which foolish vanity engenders. We see people happy whom we have not made so, and cannot endure the sight." Charlotte looked at me with a smile as she observed the emotion with which I spoke; and a tear in Friederike's eye made me proceed. "Woe unto those," I said, "who use their power over another's heart to destroy the simple pleasures it would naturally enjoy! All the gifts, all the attentions in the world cannot compensate for the loss of that happiness which that cruel tyranny within us has destroyed." My heart was full as I spoke. The memory of many things which had happened pressed upon my mind, and filled my eyes with tears.

"We should daily repeat to ourselves," I exclaimed, "that we can do little for our friends except leave them their own joys, and increase their happiness by sharing it with them! But when souls are tormented by a violent passion, or their hearts rent with grief, is it in your power to offer them the slightest comfort?

"And when the last fatal illness seizes the being whose untimely grave you have prepared, when she lies languid and exhausted before you, her dim eyes raised to heaven, and the damp of death upon her pallid brow, then you stand at her bedside like a condemned criminal, with the bitter feeling that your whole future could not save her; and the agonizing thought haunts you that all your efforts cannot impart even a moment's strength to the departing soul, or quicken her with a moment of consolation."

As I spoke these words, the memory of a similar scene at which I had once been present fell with full force upon my heart. I put my handkerchief to my face, and left the room; I was recalled to my senses only by Charlotte's voice, reminding me that it was time to go home. With what tenderness she scolded me on the way for the too eager interest I took in everything! It would destroy me, she said, and I ought to spare myself. O, Angel! I will live for your sake.

July 6

She is still with her dying friend, and is always the same helpful and lovely creature whose presence softens pain, and brings happiness wherever she goes. She went out yesterday with little Marianne and Amalie: I knew of it, and went to meet them; and we walked together. After about an hour and a half, we returned to the town. We stopped at the spring I am so fond of, and which is now a thousand times dearer to me than ever: Charlotte sat down by the low wall, and we gathered about her. I looked round, and recalled the time when my heart was all alone. "Beloved spring," I said, "since that time I have not come to enjoy cool repose by thy fresh stream; I have passed thee with scarcely a glance." I looked down, and observed Amalie coming up the steps with a glass of water. I turned to-wards Charlotte, and felt deeply what she means to me. Amalie approached with the glass. Marianne wanted to take it from her. "No!" cried the child with the sweetest expression, "Charlotte must drink first."

The goodness and simplicity with which this was uttered so charmed me that I sought to express my feelings by catching up the child and kissing her heartily. But she was frightened and began to cry. "You should not do that," said Charlotte. I was perplexed. "Come, little one," she continued, taking her hand and leading her down the steps, "wash yourself quickly in the fresh water, and it won't hurt." I stood and watched the little dear rubbing her cheeks with her wet hands, in the fervent belief that all the impurities would be washed off by the miraculous water, and that she would surely be spared the disgrace of an ugly beard. Even though Charlotte said it would do, she continued to wash with all her might, as if she thought too much were better than too little—I assure you, Wilhelm, I never attended a baptism with greater reverence; and when Charlotte came up, I could have fallen on my knees as before a prophet who has washed away the sins of his people.

In the evening I could not help telling the story to a man who, I thought, possessed some natural feeling, because he was a man of understanding. But what a mistake I made! He maintained it was very wrong of Charlotte—that we should not deceive children, that such fanciful explanations occasion countless mistakes and superstitions from which we should protect the young. It occurred to me, then, that this very man had had his child baptized only a week before; so I said nothing, but silently kept my belief that we should deal with children as God deals with us—we are happiest under the influence of innocent delusions.

July 8

What a child I am to be so solicitous about a look! What a child I am! We had been to Wahlheim: the ladies went in a carriage; but during our walks I thought I saw in Charlotte's black eyes—

I am a fool—but forgive me! you should see them, those eyes. However, to be brief (for I can hardly keep my own eyes open), when the ladies stepped into their carriage again, young W., Seldstadt, Audran, and I were standing about the door. They were a merry lot of fellows, all laughing and joking together. I watched Charlotte's eyes. They wandered from one to the other; but on me they did not light—on me, who stood there motionless, on me who alone saw her. My heart bade her a thousand adieus, but she noticed me not. The carriage drove off, and my eyes filled with tears. I looked after her: suddenly I saw Charlotte's bonnet leaning out of the window, as she turned to look back—was it at me? My dear friend, I know not; and in this uncertainty I am suspended; but that is also my consolation: perhaps she turned to look at me. Perhaps! Good night—what a child I am!

July 10

You should see how foolish I look in company when her name is mentioned, and particularly when I am asked how I like her. How I like her!—I detest the phrase. What sort of creature must he be who merely likes Charlotte, whose whole heart and senses are not entirely absorbed by her? Like her! Someone asked me the other day how I liked Ossian.

July 11

Mrs. M. is very ill. I pray for her because I share Charlotte's sufferings. I see Charlotte occasionally at a friend's house, and today she told me the strangest thing. Old Mr. M. is a greedy, miserly fellow who has long worried his wife and kept her on an unreasonably strict allowance; but she has always been able to manage. A few days ago, when the doctor knew that there was little chance of her recovery, she sent for her husband—Charlotte was present—and said this to him: "I have something to confess which, after my death, may cause trouble and confusion. I have always managed your household as frugally and economically as possible, but you must forgive me for having deceived you for thirty years. At the beginning of our married life you allowed a small sum for the kitchen and other household expenses. When our establishment increased and our property grew larger, I could not persuade you to increase the weekly allowance in proportion; in short, you know that when our household cost most, you expected me to supply everything with seven florins a week. I took the money from you without saying anything, but made up the weekly deficiency from the receipts—as nobody would suspect your wife of robbing the till. But I have wasted nothing, and should have been content to meet my eternal Judge without this confession, if I did not know that whoever looks after the house when I am gone will not be able to manage, and that you might insist that your allowance had been quite sufficient for your first wife."

I talked with Charlotte of the incredible blindness of men; how anyone could avoid suspecting some deception, when seven florins were allowed, to defray expenses twice as great. But I have myself known people who believed, without any visible astonishment, that their house possessed the prophet's never-failing cruse of oil.

<hr>

July 13

No, I am not deceived. In her black eyes I read a genuine interest in me and in my life. Yes, I feel it; and I can believe my own heart which tells me—dare I say it?—dare I pronounce the divine words?—that she loves me !

That she loves me! How the idea exalts me in my own eyes! And—as you can understand my feelings, I may say it to you—how I worship myself since she loves me!

Is this presumption, or is it an awareness of the truth? I do not know the man able to supplant me in the heart of Charlotte; and yet when she speaks of her betrothed with so much warmth and affection, I feel like the soldier who has been stripped of his honors and titles, and deprived of his sword.

———————◆———————

July 16

How my heart beats when by accident I touch her finger, or my feet meet hers under the table! I draw back as from a flame; but a secret force impels me forward again, and I become disordered. Her innocent, pure heart never knows what agony these little familiarities inflict upon me. Sometimes when we are talking she lays her hand upon mine, and in the eagerness of conversation comes closer to me, and her divine breath comes to my lips—I feel as if lightning had struck me, and I could sink into the earth. And yet, Wilhelm, with all this heavenly confidence—if I should ever dare—you understand. No! my heart is not so depraved; it is weak, weak enough—but is that not a kind of depravity?

She is sacred to me. All passion is silenced in her presence; I do not know what I feel when I am near her. It is as if my soul beat in every nerve of my body. There is a melody which she plays on the piano with the touch of an angel—so simple is it, and yet so lofty! It is her favorite air; and when she strikes the first note, all worry and sorrow disappear in a moment.

I believe every word that is said of the ancient magic of music. How her simple song enchants me! And how she knows when to play it! Sometimes, when I feel like shooting a bullet into my head, she sings that air; the gloom and madness are dispersed, and I breathe freely again.

Wilhelm, what is the world to our hearts without love? It is a magic lantern without light. You have but to set up the light within, and the brightest pictures are thrown on the white screen; and if that were all there is, fleeting shadows, we are yet happy, when, like children, we behold them and are transported with the wonderful sight. I have not been able to see Charlotte today. I was prevented by company from which I could not disengage myself. What was I to do? I sent my servant to her house, that I might at least see somebody today who had been near her. Oh, the impatience with which I waited for his return, the joy with which I welcomed him! I should have liked to hold him in my arms and kiss him, if I had not been ashamed.

It is said that the Bonona stone, when it is placed in the sun, attracts the rays and for a time appears luminous in the dark. So was it with me and this servant. The idea that her eyes had dwelt on his countenance, his cheek, his coat buttons, the collar of his surtout, made them all inestimably dear to me, so that at the moment I would not have parted with him for a thousand crowns. His presence made me so happy! For heaven's sake, Wilhelm, don't laugh at me! Can that be a delusion which makes us so happy?

"I shall see her today!" I say to myself with delight, when I rise in the morning, and happily look out at the bright, beautiful sun. "I shall see her!" And then I have no further wish for the rest of the day; all, all is focused in that one thought.

July 20

I cannot quite agree to your proposal that I should accompany the ambassador to * * *. I do not like subordination; and we all know that he is a disagreeable person. You say my mother wishes me to be employed. I could not help laughing at that. Am I not sufficiently employed? And is it not in the end the same, whether I count peas or lentils? The world runs on from one folly to another; and the man who, purely for the sake of others, and without any passion or inner compulsion of his own, toils after wealth or dignity, or any other phantom, is simply a fool.

July 24

You insist so often on my not neglecting my drawing that it would be as well for me to say nothing as to confess how little I have lately done.

I never felt happier, I never understood Nature better, even down to the stones or smallest blade of grass; and yet I am unable to express myself; the creative power of my imagination is so weak, everything seems to swim and float before me, so that I cannot make a clear, bold outline. But I think I should succeed better if I had clay or wax to model. I shall try, if this state of mind continues much longer, and will take to modeling. if I make only cakes.

I have begun Charlotte's portrait three times, and have as often made a fool of myself. This is the more annoying, as I was formerly very successful in catching likenesses. I have since sketched her profile, and must content myself with that.

------◆------

July 26

Yes, dear Charlotte! I will take care of everything as you wish. Do give me more commissions, the more the better. Only do me one favor; use no more writing sand with the little notes you send me. Today I quickly raised your letter to my lips, and it set my teeth on edge.

------◆------

July 26

I have often resolved not to see her so frequently. But who could keep such a resolution? Every day I succumb to temptation, and promise faithfully that tomorrow I will really stay away; but when tomorrow comes, I find some irresistible reason for seeing her; and before I can account for it, I am with her again. Either she said on the previous evening, "Be sure to call tomorrow, won't you?"—and who could stay away?—or she gives me some commission, and I think it proper to take her the answer in person; or the day is lovely, and I walk to Wahlheim; and when I am there, it is only half an hour to her. I am within the enchanted atmosphere, and suddenly find myself at her side. My grandmother used to tell us a story of a mountain of loadstone. Any ships that came near it were instantly deprived of their ironwork; the nails flew to the mountain, and the unhappy crew perished amidst the debris of the planks.

July 30

Albert has arrived, and I must go. Were he the best and noblest of men, and I in every respect his inferior, I could not endure to see him in possession of such perfection. Possession!— Enough, Wilhelm—her betrothed is here—a fine, worthy fellow, whom one cannot help liking. Fortunately I was not present at their meeting. It would have broken my heart! And he is so considerate; he has not given Charlotte one kiss in my presence. Heaven reward him for it! I must love him for the respect with which he treats her. He shows a regard for me; but I suspect I am more indebted for that to Charlotte than to his own fancy for me. Women have a delicate tact in such matters, and rightly so. They cannot always succeed in keeping two rivals on terms with each other; but when they do, they are the only gainers.

I cannot help respecting Albert. The calm of his temper contrasts strongly with the impetuosity of mine, which I cannot conceal. He has a great deal of feeling, and knows what he possesses in Charlotte. He is free from ill-humor, which you know is the fault I detest most.

He regards me as a man of sense; and my attachment to Charlotte, and the interest I take in all that concerns her, augment his triumph and his love. I shall not inquire whether he does not at times tease her with petty jealousy; I know that I in his place should not be entirely free from such feelings.

But, be that as it may, my pleasure with Charlotte is over. Call it folly or infatuation, what matters a name? The thing speaks for itself. Before Albert came, I knew all that I know now. I knew I could make no pretensions to her, nor did I make any—that is, as far as it was possible to be without desire in the presence of so much loveliness. And now look at me, the silly creature, staring at the other fellow coming along and taking the girl away.

I grit my teeth and feel infinite scorn for those who tell me to be resigned, because it cannot be helped. Let me get away from these stuffed gentlemen! I ramble through the woods; and when I return to Charlotte, and find Albert sitting by her side in the arbor in the garden, I can't bear it, behave like a fool, and indulge in a thousand absurdities. "For Heaven's sake," Charlotte said today, "no more scenes like those of last night! You frighten me when you are so violent." Between ourselves, I only wait until he is busy elsewhere, and I am out there in no time, delighted when I find her alone.

———◆———

August 8

Believe me, Wilhelm, I did not mean you when I spoke so severely of those who always advise resignation to inevitable fate. I did not think you would have any such ideas. Of course you are right. Only remember one thing: in this world it is seldom a question of "either . . . or." There are as many alternatives of conduct and opinion as there are turns of feature between an aquiline nose and a flat one.

You must, therefore, permit me to concede your entire argument, and yet contrive to find a way somewhere between the "either . . . or."

I hear you say: "Either you have hopes of obtaining Charlotte, or you have none. Well, in the one case, pursue your course, and press on to the fulfillment of your wishes. In the other, be a man, and try to get rid of a miserable passion, which will enervate and destroy you." My dear friend, this is well said—and easily said.

But would you ask a wretched being, whose life is slowly wasting under a lingering disease, to do away with himself by the stroke of a dagger? Does not the very disorder which consumes his strength deprive him of the courage to effect his own deliverance?

You may answer me, if you please, with a similar analogy: "Who would not prefer the amputation of an arm to the risk of losing his life by hesitation and procrastination?" I know . . . let us not fence with metaphors.

Enough! There are moments, Wilhelm, when I could rise up and shake it all off, and when, if I only knew where, I think I would go away.

———◆———

The same evening

Today I found my diary, which I have neglected for some time; and I am amazed how deliberately I have entangled myself step by step. To have recognized my situation so clearly, and yet to have acted like a child! Even now I see it all plainly, and yet seem to have no thought of acting more wisely.

———◆———

August 10

If I were not a fool, I could lead the happiest and most delightful life here. So many agreeable circumstances, all designed to please a man's heart, are seldom to be found. Alas! I feel it so clearly—the heart alone makes our happiness! To be admitted into this most charming family, to be loved by the father as a son, by the children as a father, and by Charlotte!—then Albert in all his generosity, who never disturbs my happiness by any appearance of ill-humor, receiving me with sincere affection, and loving me, next to Charlotte, better than all the world! Wilhelm, you would be delighted to hear us on our walks, talking about Charlotte. Nothing in the world can be more absurd than our relationship, and yet it often moves me to tears.

He tells me sometimes of her wonderful mother; how, on her deathbed, she entrusted her house and children to Charlotte, and asked him to look after her; how, since that time, a new spirit had taken possession of her; how, in her concern for their welfare, she became a real mother to them; how every moment of her time is devoted to some labor of love in their behalf— and yet her gaiety and cheerfulness has never left her. I walk by his side, pluck flowers by the way, arrange them carefully into a nosegay, fling them into the brook, and watch them as they float gently downstream. I forget whether I told you that Albert is to remain here. He has received a court appointment, with a very good salary; I understand he is in high favor there. I have met few persons so regular and conscientious as he is in his profession.

August 12

Certainly Albert is the best fellow in the world. I had a strange scene with him yesterday. I went to take leave of him, for I had taken it into my head to spend a few days in these hills from where I now write to you. As I was walking up and down his room, my eye fell upon his pistols. "Lend me those pistols," said I, "for my journey." "By all means," he replied, "if you will take the trouble to load them; they only hang there pro forma." I took down one of them, and he continued: "Ever since I nearly paid for my extreme caution, I will have nothing to do with these things." I was curious to hear the story. "I was staying," said he, "some three months ago at a friend's house in the country. I had a brace of pistols with me, unloaded; and I slept without anxiety. One rainy afternoon I was sitting by myself, doing nothing, when it occurred to me—I do not know how—that the house might be attacked, that we might require the pistols, that we might—in short, you know how we sometimes imagine things when we have nothing better to do. I gave the pistols to the servant to clean and load. He was dallying with the maids and trying to frighten them, when the pistol went off—God knows how! The ramrod was still in the barrel; and it went straight through the ball of the right thumb of one of the girls and shattered it. I had to endure her lamentations and pay the surgeon's bill; so, since that time, I have kept my weapons unloaded. My dear fellow, what is the use of prudence? We can never guard against all possible dangers. However,"—now you must know I am very fond of him until he says "however"; is it not self-evident that every universal rule must have its exceptions? But he is so exceedingly anxious to justify himself that if he thinks he has said anything too precipitate or too general or only half true, he never stops qualifying, modifying, and extenuating till at last he appears to have said nothing at all. On this occasion Albert was deeply immersed in his subject; I finally ceased to listen to him, and became lost in reverie. With a sudden motion I pointed the mouth of the pistol to my forehead, over the right eye. "What are you doing?" cried Albert, turning the pistol away. "It is not loaded," said I. "Even so," he asked with impatience, "what is the meaning of this? I cannot imagine how a man can be so mad as to shoot himself; the very idea of it shocks me."

"Oh, you people!" I said, "why should you always have to

label an action and call it mad or wise, good or bad? What does it all mean? Have you fathomed the motives of our actions? Can you explain the causes and make them inevitable? If you could, you would be less hasty with your 'labels.' "

"But you will admit," said Albert, "that some actions are vicious, let them spring from whatever motives they may." I granted it, and shrugged my shoulders.

"Still," I continued, "there are some exceptions here too. Theft is a crime; but the man who commits it from extreme poverty to save his family from starvation, does he deserve pity or punishment? Who shall throw the first stone at a husband who in just resentment sacrifices his faithless wife and her perfidious seducer; or at the young girl who in an hour of rapture forgets herself in the overwhelming joys of love? Even our laws, cold and pedantic as they are, relent in such cases, and withhold their punishment."

"That is quite another thing," said Albert, "because a man under the influence of violent passion loses all reasoning power and is regarded as drunk or insane."

"Oh, you rationalists," I replied, smiling. "Passion! Drunkenness! Madness! You moral creatures, so calm and so righteous! You abhor the drunken man, and detest the eccentric; you pass by, like the Levite, and thank God, like the Pharisee, that you are not like one of them. I have been drunk more than once, my passions have always bordered on madness; I am not ashamed to confess it; I have learned in my own way that all extraordinary men who have done great and improbable things have ever been decried by the world as drunk or insane. And in ordinary life, too, is it not intolerable that no one can undertake anything noble or generous without having everybody shout, 'That fellow is drunk, he is mad'? Shame on you, ye sages!"

"Here you go again," said Albert; "you always exaggerate, and in this matter you are undoubtedly wrong; we were speaking of suicide, which you compare with great actions, when actually it is impossible to regard it as anything but weakness. It is much easier to die than to bear a life of misery with fortitude."

I was on the point of breaking off the conversation, for nothing puts me off so completely as when someone utters a wretched commonplace when I am talking from the depths of my heart. However, I controlled myself, for I had often heard the same observation with sufficient vexation; I answered him, therefore, with some heat, "You call this a weakness—don't be led astray by appearances. When a nation which has long groaned under the intolerable yoke of a tyrant rises at last and throws off its chains, do you call that weakness? The man who, to save his house from the flames, finds his physical strength redoubled, so that he can lift burdens with ease which normally he could scarcely move; he who under the rage of an insult attacks and overwhelms half a dozen of his enemies—are these to be called weak? My friend, if a display of energy be strength, how can the highest exertion of it be a weakness?"

Albert looked at me and said, "Do forgive me, but I do not see that the examples you have produced bear any relation to the question." "That may be," I answered; "I have often been told that my method of argument borders a little on the absurd. But let us see if we cannot place the matter in another light by inquiring what may be a man's state of mind who resolves to free himself from the burden of life—a burden which often seems so pleasant to bear. Surely, we are justified in discussing a subject such as this only in so far as we can put ourselves in another man's situation."

"Human nature," I continued, "has its limits. It can endure a certain degree of joy, sorrow, and pain, but collapses as soon as this is exceeded. The question, therefore, is not whether a man is strong or weak, but whether he is able to endure the measure of his suffering, moral or physical; and in my opinion it is just as absurd to call a man a coward who kills himself as to call a man a coward who dies of a malignant fever."

44

"Paradox, all paradox!" cried Albert. "Not so paradoxical as you imagine," I replied. "You admit that we call a disease mortal when Nature is so severely attacked and her strength so far exhausted that she cannot possibly recover, no matter what the change that may take place.

"Now, my friend, apply this to the mind; observe a man in his natural, confined condition; consider how ideas work upon him, and how impressions affect him, till at length a violent passion seizes him, destroys all his powers of calm reflection, and utterly ruins him.

"It is in vain that a man of sound mind and cool temper recognizes the condition of such a wretched being, in vain that he counsels him. Just as a healthy man cannot impart his strength to an invalid."

Albert thought this too general. I reminded him about a girl who had drowned herself a short time previously, and I related her story.

"She was a good creature, who had grown up in the narrow sphere of her domestic chores and weekly appointed labor; one who knew no pleasure beyond a walk in the company of her friends on Sundays, dressed in her best clothes, which she had got together gradually; or perhaps going to a dance now and then during the holidays, and chatting away her spare hours with a neighbor, discussing the scandals or the quarrels of the village—trifles sufficient to occupy her heart. At length the warmth of her nature is aroused by unfamiliar desires. She is flattered by the attentions of men; her former pleasures seem to her more and more insipid, till eventually she meets a young man to whom she is attracted by a strange, new feeling; upon him she now rests all her hopes; she forgets the world around her; she sees, hears, desires nothing but him, and him only. He alone occupies all her thoughts. Unspoiled by the empty indulgence of enervating vanity, her affection moving steadily towards its object, she hopes to be his, and to realize, in an everlasting union with him, all that happiness which she sought, all that bliss for which she longed. His repeated promises confirm her hopes; embraces and endearments, which increase the ardor of her desires, overpower her soul. She floats in a dim, delusive anticipation of her happiness; and her feelings become excited to their utmost tension. She stretches out her arms finally to embrace the object of all her wishes—and her lover abandons her. Stunned and bewildered, she stands upon a precipice. All is darkness around her. No prospect, no hope, no consolation—forsaken by him in whom her existence was centered! She sees nothing of the world before her, thinks nothing of the many others who might fill the void in her heart; she feels herself deserted, forsaken by all the world; and, unseeing and impelled by the agony in her soul, she plunges into the deep, to end her sufferings in the broad embrace of death. You see, Albert, this is the story of thousands; and now tell me, is not this a case of physical infirmity? Nature can find no way out of the labyrinth of confusion and contradiction; and the poor creature must die.

"Shame on him who can look on calmly and say, 'Foolish girl! She should have waited; she should have let time wear off the impression; her despair would have been eased, and she would have found another lover to comfort her.' One might as well say, 'The fool, to die of a fever! Why did he not wait till his strength was restored, till his blood became calm? All would have gone well, and he would have been alive now.'"

Albert, who could not even now see the justice of the comparison, offered some further objections, amongst others, that I had taken the case of a mere ignorant girl. But how a rational being of sense, of more understanding and experience, could be excused, he was unable to comprehend. "My friend!" I exclaimed, "a man is a man; and whatever be the extent of his reasoning powers, they are of little avail when passion rages within, and he feels himself confined by the narrow limits of human nature. Rather—but let us talk of this some other time," I said, and took my hat. My heart was over full; and we parted without having understood each other. How rare in this world is understanding!

———◆———

August 15

There can be no doubt that in this world nothing makes us indispensable to each other but love alone. I know that Charlotte could not lose me without a pang, and the children will take it for granted that I should visit them every morning. I went this afternoon to tune Charlotte's piano. But I could not do it, for the little ones insisted on my telling them a story; and Charlotte herself asked me to satisfy them. I gave them their supper, and they are now as fully contented with me as with Charlotte; and I told them my favorite tale of the princess who was waited upon by hands. I learn a great deal doing this and am surprised at the impression my stories create. If I sometimes invent a minor episode which I forget the next time, they are quick to remind me that the story was different before; so that I now practice reciting them unchanged in the same singsong tone which never changes. I learn by this how much an author injures his work by altering it in a second edition, even though it may be improved from a literary point of view. The first impression is readily received. We are so constituted that we believe the most incredible things; and, once they are engraved upon the memory, woe to him who would endeavor to erase them.

———◆———

August 18

Must it ever be thus—that the source of our happiness must also be the fountain of our misery? The rich and ardent feeling

47

which filled my heart with a love of Nature, overwhelmed me with a torrent of delight, and brought all paradise before me, has now become an insupportable torment—a demon which perpetually pursues me. When I used to gaze from these rocks upon the mountains across the river and upon the green valley before me, and saw everything around budding and bursting; the hills clothed from foot to peak with tall, thick trees; the valleys in all their variety, shaded with the loveliest woods; and the river gently gliding along among the whispering reeds, mirroring the clouds which the soft evening breeze wafted across the sky—when I heard the groves about me melodious with the music of birds, and saw the million swarms of insects dancing in the last golden beams of the sun, whose setting rays awoke the humming beetles from their grassy beds, while the subdued tumult around me drew my attention to the ground, and I there observed the hard rock giving nourishment to the dry moss, while the heather flourished upon the arid sands below me—all this conveyed to me the holy fire which animates all Nature, and filled and glowed within my heart. I felt myself exalted by this overflowing fullness to the perception of the Godhead, and the glorious forms of an infinite universe stirred within my soul! Stupendous mountains encompassed me, abysses yawned at my feet, and cataracts fell headlong down before me; rivers rolled through the plains below, and rocks and mountains resounded from afar. In the depths of the earth I saw the mysterious powers at work; on its surface, and beneath the heavens there teemed ten thousand living creatures. Everything is alive with an infinite variety of forms; mankind safeguards itself in little houses and settles and rules in its own way over the wide universe. Poor fool! in whose petty estimation all things are little. From the inaccessible mountains, across the wilderness which no mortal foot has trod, far as the confines of the unknown ocean, breathes the spirit of the eternal Creator; and every speck of dust which He has made finds favor in His sight—Ah, how often at that time has the flight of a crane, soaring above my head, inspired me with the desire to be transported to the shores of the immeasurable ocean, there to quaff the pleasures of life from the foaming goblet of the Infinite, and to realize, if but for a moment with the confined powers of my soul, the bliss of that Creator Who accomplishes all things in Himself, and through Himself!

My dear friend, the mere recollection of those hours consoles me. Even the effort to recall those ineffable emotions, and give them utterance, exalts my soul above itself, and makes me feel doubly the intensity of my present anguish.

It is as if a curtain had been drawn from before my eyes, and, instead of prospects of eternal life, the abyss of an ever-open grave yawned before me. Can we say of anything that it *is* when all passes away—when time, with the speed of a storm, carries all things onward—and our transitory existence, hurried along by the torrent, is swallowed up by the waves or dashed against the rocks? There is not a moment but consumes you and yours —not a moment in which you do not yourself destroy something. The most innocent walk costs thousands of poor insects their lives; one step destroys the delicate structures of the ant and turns a little world into chaos. No; it is not the great and rare catastrophes of the world, the floods which sweep away villages, the earthquakes that swallow up our towns, that affect me. My heart is wasted by the thought of that destructive power which lies latent in every part of universal Nature. Nature has formed nothing that does not destroy itself, and everything near it. And so, surrounded by earth and air and all the active forces, I stagger on with anguished heart; the universe to me is an ever devouring, ever ruminating monster.

August 21

In vain do I stretch out my arms towards her when I awaken in the morning from my troubled dreams. In vain I seek her at night in my bed, when an innocent dream has happily deceived me, and I thought that I was sitting near her in the fields, holding her hand and covering it with countless kisses. And when I feel for her in the half confusion of sleep, and awaken, tears flow from my oppressed heart; and, bereft of all comfort, I weep over my future woes.

August 22

What misery, Wilhelm! My energies have degenerated into restless inaction. I cannot be idle, and yet I am unable to set to work. My powers of imagination are gone; I have no longer any feeling for the beauties of Nature, and books are distasteful to me. Once we give ourselves up, we are lost. Many a time I wish I were a common laborer, so that when I awake in the morning I might at least have one clear prospect, one pursuit, one hope, for the day which has dawned. I often envy Albert when I see him buried in a heap of papers and documents, and I fancy that I should be happy were I in his place. This feeling has so often come over me that I have been on the point of writing to you and to the minister for the appointment at the embassy, which you assure me I might obtain. I believe I should have a chance. The minister has long shown a regard for me, and has frequently urged me to seek employment. But it is the whim of an hour only. Then the fable of the horse recurs to me. Weary of its freedom, it let itself be saddled and bridled, and was ridden to death for its pains. I know not what to do. For is not this craving for change the consequence of an impatient spirit which will forever pursue me?

If my misery could be cured at all, it would certainly be cured here among these people. This is my birthday, and early in the morning I received a package from Albert. As I opened it, I found one of the pink ribbons which Charlotte wore in her dress the first time I saw her, and which I had several times asked her to give me. With it were two volumes in duodecimo of Wetstein's Homer—a book I had often wanted to own, to save me the trouble of carrying the large Ernesti edition with me on my walks. You see how they anticipate my wishes, how well they understand all those little attentions of friendship, so superior to the expensive presents of the great, which are humiliating. I kissed the ribbon a thousand times, and in every breath inhaled the memory of those happy and irrevocable days, which filled me with the keenest joy. Such, Wilhelm, is our fate. I do not complain; the flowers of life are but illusions. How many fade away and leave no trace; how few yield any fruit; and the fruit itself, how rarely does it ripen! And yet there are flowers enough; should we let the little that does really ripen, rot, decay and perish unenjoyed?

Farewell! This is a glorious summer. I often climb into the trees in Charlotte's orchard, and with a fruit picker bring down the pears that hang on the highest branches; she stands below, and takes them as I hand them to her.

Foolish fellow that I am! Why do I deceive myself? What is to come of all this wild, endless passion? I cannot pray except to her. My imagination sees nothing but her; nothing matters except what has to do with her. In this state of mind I enjoy many happy hours, till at length I feel compelled to tear myself away from her. Ah, Wilhelm, to what lengths does my heart often drive me! When I have spent several hours in her company, till I feel completely absorbed by her figure, her grace, the divine expression of her thoughts, my mind becomes deeply excited, my sight grows dim, my hearing confused, my breathing oppressed as if by the hand of an assassin, and my beating heart seeks relief for my aching senses. I am sometimes uncertain whether I really exist. If in such moments I find no sympathy, and Charlotte does not allow me to enjoy the melancholy consolation of bathing her hand in my tears, I tear myself from her and roam through the country, climb some precipitous cliff, or make a path through a trackless wood, where I am wounded and torn by thorns and briers; and there I find some relief. Sometimes I lie down on the way, overcome with fatigue and thirst; sometimes, late in the night, when the full moon stands above me in the lonely woods, I sit on a crooked tree to rest my weary limbs, and there, exhausted and worn, I fall asleep in the subdued light. Oh Wilhelm! the hermit's cell, his sackcloth and belt of thorns would be relief compared with what I suffer. Adieu! I see no end to this wretchedness except the grave.

September 3

I must away. Thank you, Wilhelm, for confirming my wavering purpose. For a whole fortnight I have thought of leaving her. I must. She is in town again, visiting a friend. And Albert—yes—I must away.

September 10

Oh, what a night, Wilhelm! Henceforth I can bear anything. I shall not see her again. Oh, why cannot I fall on your neck, and with floods of tears and raptures convey to you all the passions which overwhelm my heart! Here I sit gasping for breath, and struggling to calm myself. I wait for day, and at dawn the horses are to be at the door.

And she is sleeping calmly, little suspecting that she has seen me for the last time. I am free. I have had the courage, in a conversation of two hours, not to betray my intention. Oh, Wilhelm, what a conversation it was!

Albert had promised to come with Charlotte to the garden immediately after supper. I stood on the terrace under the tall chestnuts and watched the setting sun. I saw it sink for the last time over this delightful valley and gentle stream. I had often visited the same spot with Charlotte, and watched that glorious sight; and now—I walked up and down the avenue which was so dear to me. A secret sympathy had frequently drawn me thither even before I knew Charlotte; and we were delighted when, early in our acquaintance, we discovered that we loved the same spot, which is as romantic as any that the gardener's art has ever produced.

From between the chestnuts there is a broad view. I remember that I have mentioned all this in a previous letter, and have described the tall mass of beech trees at the end, and how the avenue grows darker and darker as it winds its way among them, till it ends in an enclosure which has all the mysterious charm of solitude. I can recall the strange feeling of melancholy which came over me the first time I entered that dark retreat, at bright midday. I seemed to feel even then that it would some day be the scene of so much happiness and misery!

I had spent half an hour absorbed in the bittersweet thoughts of parting and seeing her again, when I heard them coming up the terrace. I ran to meet them. I trembled as I took her hand and kissed it. When we reached the top of the terrace, the moon rose from behind the wooded hill. We talked about many things, and almost without noticing it approached the secluded spot. Charlotte entered, and sat down, Albert beside her. I did the same, but I was so excited that I could not remain seated. I got up and stood before her, then walked to and fro, and sat down again. I was restless and miserable. Charlotte drew our attention to the beautiful effect of the moonlight, which threw a silver hue over the terrace in front of the beech trees. It was a glorious sight, all the more striking because of the complete darkness which surrounded the spot where we were. We remained silent; and after a while Charlotte said, "Whenever I walk by moonlight, it brings to my mind my beloved and departed friends, and I am filled with thoughts of death and afterlife. We shall live, Werther," she continued, with a firm but feeling voice; "but shall we know one another again? What do you think? What do you say?"

"Charlotte," I said, as I took her hand in mine, and my eyes filled with tears, "we shall see each other again—here and hereafter." I could say no more. Why, Wilhelm, should she put this question to me just at the moment when the anguish of our parting filled my heart?

"And," she continued, "do those departed ones know of us

down here? Do they know when we are well that we recall their memory with the fondest love? In the quiet of evening, the shade of my mother always hovers round me, when I sit in the midst of her children, my children, when they are assembled about me as they used to be with her; and then I raise my anxious eyes to Heaven, and wish she could look down upon us and see how I keep the promise I made to her in her last moments on her deathbed to be a mother to her children. With what emotion do I cry out, 'Forgive me, dearest mother, forgive me if I cannot completely take your place! I do my best. They are clothed and fed; and, still better, they are cared for and loved. Could you but see, dear saint, the peace and harmony of our life, you would praise God with the deepest feelings of gratitude, to Whom, in your last hour, you addressed such fervent prayers for our happiness.' "

This is what she said! Oh, Wilhelm, who can do justice to her words? How can the cold dead letter convey the heavenly expressions of her spirit? Albert interrupted her gently: "This affects you too deeply, dear Charlotte. I know you dwell on such recollections with deep feeling; but I implore you—" "Oh, Albert!" she continued, "I am sure you do not forget the evenings when we three used to sit at the little round table, when Father was away, and the little ones had gone to bed. You often had a good book with you but seldom read it; the conversation of that wonderful soul was more than anything else—that beautiful, bright, gentle, and yet ever-active woman. God alone knows how I have often prayed in tears that I might be like her!"

I threw myself at her feet, and covered her hand with a thousand tears. "Charlotte," I exclaimed, "God's blessing and your mother's spirit are upon you!" "Oh that you had known her!" she said, pressing my hand. "She was worthy of being known by you." I thought I should faint. Never had I received praise so magnificent. She continued: "And yet she was doomed to die in the prime of her life, when her youngest boy was six months old. Her illness was but short, she was calm and resigned; it was only for her children, especially the youngest, that she felt unhappy. When her end drew near, she asked me to bring them to her. I took them in to her. The little ones knew nothing of their approaching loss; the elder ones were overcome with grief. They stood around the bed; and she raised her hands and prayed over them; then she kissed them one after the other and sent them away. 'Be a mother to them,' she said to me. I gave her my hand. 'You are promising much, my child,' she said,—'a mother's love and a mother's eye! I have often felt, by your tears of gratitude, that you know what that means; show it to your brothers and sisters. And be as obedient and faithful to your father as a wife; you will be his comfort.' She asked for him. He had gone out to conceal his intolerable anguish—he was completely broken.

"Albert, you were in the room. She heard someone moving about, inquired who it was, and asked you to approach. She looked at us both steadily, reassured that we should be happy—happy with each other." Albert embraced her and cried, "We are happy, and we always shall be!" Even Albert, tranquil Albert, had quite lost his composure; and I was moved beyond expression.

"And this woman," she continued, "had to leave us, Werther! God, must we part with everything we hold dear in this world? Nobody felt this more deeply than the children; they cried for a long time afterward and complained that the black men had carried away their dear mama."

Charlotte rose. I was so disturbed and shaken that I could not move, and held her hand. "Let us go," she said; "it is late." She wanted to withdraw her hand, but I held it. "We shall see each other again," I cried; "we shall recognize each other under whatever conditions! I am going," I continued, "going willingly; but if I had to say forever, I could not bear it. Adieu, Charlotte; adieu, Albert. We shall meet again." "Yes; tomorrow, I suppose," she answered lightly. Tomorrow! how

I felt the word! Oh! she little knew when she drew her hand away from mine . . . They walked down the avenue. I stood gazing after them in the moonlight, then threw myself on the ground, and wept, sprang up, and ran out on the terrace, and there below in the shade of the linden trees, I saw her white frock gleaming as she disappeared near the garden gate. I stretched out my arms, and she vanished.

Book Two

WE ARRIVED here yesterday. The ambassador is indisposed, and will not go out for some days. If he were less unpleasant, all would be well. I see only too clearly that there are several trials in store for me; but courage; a light heart can bear anything. A light heart! I smile to find such a word coming from my pen. A little more lightheartedness would make me the happiest being under the sun. But must I despair of my talents and faculties, while others of far inferior gifts parade about with the utmost self-satisfaction? Gracious Providence, to Whom I owe all my powers, why didst Thou not withhold half the blessings I possess, and give me in their place self-confidence and contentment?

But patience, patience! All will yet be well; you were quite right, my friend: since I have had to associate with other people and see what they do and how they live, I have become better satisfied with myself. For this is our nature, that we are ever anxious to compare ourselves with others; and our happiness or misery depends on the things and people with whom we compare ourselves. And nothing is more dangerous than solitude; our imagination, always disposed to rise high, nourished by the fantastic images of the poets, seems to project for us a chain of beings of whom we ourselves seem the most inferior. All things appear more perfect than they really are, and all seem superior to us. This is quite natural; we feel so often our own imperfections, and imagine that we perceive in others the qualities we do not possess, attributing to them also all that we have ourselves. And then we form the idea of the perfect, happy man—but a creature of our own imagination.

But when, in spite of weakness and disappointments, we do our daily work in earnest, we shall find that with all false starts and compromises, we make better headway than others who have wind and tide with them; and there can be no greater satisfaction than to keep pace with others or outstrip them in the race.

November 26, 1771

I am beginning to find life here more tolerable, considering all circumstances. The best thing is that I am busy; and the people I meet and their different ways keep me interested. I met Count C., and I respect him more and more every day. He is a man of understanding and great discernment; although he sees farther than other people, he is not cold in his manner but can inspire and return the warmest affection. He took an interest in me on one occasion, when I had to transact some business with him. From the very first word he realized that we understood each other, and that he could talk with me as he cannot with others. His frank and open kindness to me is beyond praise. There is nothing quite so pleasing and reassuring as to find an unusual mind in sympathy with our own.

December 24, 1771

As I expected, the ambassador annoys me. He is the most punctilious fool under heaven. He does everything step by step, as meticulous as an old woman; he is a man whom it is impossible to please, because he is never pleased with himself. I like to do work quickly and, when the job is finished, leave it at that. But he is likely to return my papers to me, saying, "They will do, but you might look them over again. You can always find a better word or a more appropriate particle." I lose all patience. Not a single "and" or any other conjunction must be omitted: he hates those inversions which I am apt to overlook; and if our periods are not tuned to the official key, he cannot understand a word. It is dreadful to have to deal with such a fellow.

Count C.'s confidence is the only thing that cheers me. He told me frankly the other day that he was much displeased with the slowness and pedantry of the ambassador; that people like him make it difficult for themselves and others. "But," he added, "one has to put up with it, like a traveler who has to get across a mountain; if the mountain were not there, the road would be a good deal shorter and pleasanter, but there it is, and we must get over it."

The ambassador has noticed the Count's liking for me; this, too, annoys him, and he takes every opportunity to speak derogatorily of the Count. I naturally defend him, and that only makes matters worse. Yesterday he made me angry, for he seemed to imply criticism of me. "The Count," he said, "is a man of the world; he works easily and his style is good; but, like all literary people, he has no solid learning." He looked at me as if to see whether I had felt the blow. But he did not make me lose my temper; I despise a man who can think and act like this. However, I did make a stand, and answered with some warmth. The Count, I said, was a man entitled to respect, alike for his character and his knowledge. I had never met anyone whose mind was stored with more useful and extensive knowledge—who had, in fact, mastered such an infinite variety of subjects, and who yet retained all his feeling for the detail of ordinary business. This was all Greek to him; and I took my leave, lest more of his twaddle should annoy me further.

As a matter of fact, you people are to blame for all this—you who talked me into this and had so much to say about an "active" life. An "active" life! If the fellow who plants potatoes and takes his corn to market is not more usefully employed than I am, then let me slave ten years longer in the galleys to which I am now chained.

Oh the gilded wretchedness, the boredom among the silly people whom I meet in society here! The fighting for rank! How they watch and worry to gain precedence! What poor and contemptible passions are displayed in utter shamelessness! We have a woman here, for example, who never stops talking about her noble family and her estates. A stranger would think her a silly fool, whose head was turned by her pretensions to rank and property; but she is actually even more ridiculous— she is the daughter of a mere magistrate's clerk from this neighborhood. I cannot understand how human beings can so stupidly debase themselves.

Every day I observe more and more the folly of judging others by ourselves. I have so much trouble with myself, and my own heart is so restless, that I would be quite content to let others pursue their own ways, if they would only allow me to do the same.

What provokes me most is the extent to which distinctions of rank are carried. I know perfectly well how inevitable in-equalities of condition are; indeed, I myself derive advantages from them; but I would not have these institutions prove a barrier to the small chance of happiness which I may enjoy on this earth.

The other day, during one of my walks, I became acquainted with a Lady B. a very charming woman, who has remained natural in the midst of all this artificiality. Our first conversation pleased us both equally; and, on leaving, I asked permission to visit her. She consented so delightfully that I could hardly wait to see her again. She is not a native of this place but lives here with her aunt. The looks of the old lady are not prepossessing.

I paid her much attention, addressing the greater part of my conversation to her; and, in less than half an hour, I discovered what her niece later admitted to me, that her aged aunt, with but a small fortune and an even more limited range of understanding, enjoys no satisfaction except in the pedigree of her ancestors, no protection save in her noble birth, and no enjoyment but in looking down from her height over the heads of the humbler citizens. In her youth she was, no doubt, handsome, and probably spent her time inflicting her caprices on many a poor youth; in her later years she submitted to the yoke of a veteran officer, who, in return for her person and her small independence, spent with her what I may call her brass age. He is dead; and she is now a widow, and deserted. She spends her iron age alone and nobody would look at her if her niece were not so enchanting.

January 8, 1772

What strange beings they are, whose thoughts are completely occupied with etiquette and ceremony, who for years devote all their mental and physical energies to the task of getting one step ahead, and of trying to move up one place at the table! Not that they have nothing else to do; on the contrary, as they go to infinite trouble for such petty trifles, they have no time for more important matters. Last week a quarrel arose at a sleighing party, and our amusement was spoiled.

The silly creatures cannot see that it is not place which constitutes real greatness; the man who occupies the first place seldom plays the principal part. How often are kings governed by their ministers, and ministers by their secretaries! Who is really the chief? He, it seems to me, who can see through the others, and possesses strength or skill enough to make their power or passions serve his own designs.

I must write to you, dear Charlotte, from the tap room of this poor country inn, where I have taken shelter from a severe storm. As long as I lived in that wretched place, D., among strangers—strangers to this heart—I never felt at any time that I must write to you; but now in this cottage, in this solitude, the world shut out, with the snow and hail beating against the windowpanes, you are my first thought. The moment I entered, you came to my mind, and I remembered you—O Charlotte, our sacred, tender memories! Gracious Heaven, that happy moment of our first meeting!

If you could see me now, dear Charlotte, in the whirl of dissipation—how my mind dries up, and my heart is never really full! Not one single moment of happiness: nothing! nothing touches me. I stand, as it were, before the puppet-show; I see the little puppets move, and I ask myself whether it is not an optical illusion. I am amused by these puppets, or rather, I am myself one of them; I sometimes grasp my neighbor's wooden hand, and withdraw with a shudder. In the evening I resolve to enjoy the next morning's sunrise, but I remain in bed; during the day I promise myself a walk by moonlight; but I stay at home. I don't know why I get up nor why I go to sleep.

The leaven which animated my life is gone; the charm which cheered me in the gloom of night, and aroused me from my morning slumbers, is no longer with me.

I have found but one person here to interest me, a Lady B. She resembles you, dear Charlotte, if anyone can possibly resemble you. "Ah!" you will say, "he has learned how to pay compliments." Yes, this is partly true. I have been very well behaved lately; I can't help it; I have developed a good deal of wit; and the ladies say that no one understands flattery better (or lies, you will add; since the one invariably accompanies the other. Do you see?). But I must tell you of Lady B. She is a real person, with lovely deep blue eyes. Her rank is a torment to her, and of course satisfies none of her desires. She longs to get away from this whirl of fashion, and we often picture to ourselves a life of undisturbed happiness in a world of idyllic peace; and then we speak of you, dearest Charlotte; and she has to listen to my praises of you; no, she doesn't have to, she likes to hear me speak of you, and loves you.

Oh that I were sitting at your feet in that familiar little room, with the children playing around us! If they became troublesome to you, I would tell them some weird story; and then they would crowd round me quickly.

The sun is setting magnificently over the snow-covered country; the storm is over, and I must return to my cage. Adieu! Is Albert with you? and what is he . . . ? God forgive the question.

February 8

For a week now we have had the most wretched weather; but this is a blessing to me; every lovely day I have had here has been thoroughly spoiled by someone or other. As long as we have rain, sleet, frost and storm, I congratulate myself that it cannot be worse indoors than outside, nor worse outside than within. When the sun rises bright in the morning and promises a glorious day, I can't help saying, "There, now, they have another gift from Heaven, which they will be sure to spoil!" They destroy everything—health, reputation, happiness, amusement; and they do it through folly, lack of understanding or narrow-mindedness, and always, if you are to believe them, with the best of intentions. Sometimes I could implore them, on my bended knees, not to be so furiously determined to destroy themselves.

I am afraid that my ambassador and I shall not get along together much longer. He is quite insufferable. His manner of doing business is so ridiculous that I often cannot help contradicting him and doing things my own way; and then, of course, he disapproves. He complained of me lately on this account at court; and the minister reprimanded me—gently, to be sure—but still, he did reprimand me. I was about to submit my resignation when I received a private letter from him,[1] which I accepted with the greatest respect for the high, noble, and generous spirit which had dictated it. He tried to soothe my excessive sensibility, respected my rather exaggerated ideas of duty, of good example, and of perseverance in business, as the fruit of my youthful ardor—qualities which he did not seek to eliminate, but only to moderate, so that they might have their proper play and be productive of good. I am now at rest for another week, and no longer at variance with myself. Contentment and peace of mind are wonderful things; I only wish, dear friend, that these precious jewels were a little less frail.

February 20

God bless you, my dear friends, and may he grant you that happiness which he denies to me!

---

[1] Out of respect for this excellent man this letter and another one which is mentioned later on have not been included in the present collection. It seemed unlikely that even the warmest gratitude of the reading public would excuse such an impropriety.

I thank you, Albert, for having deceived me. I was waiting to hear when your wedding day was to be; I intended on that day solemnly to take down Charlotte's silhouette from the wall, and to bury it among my other papers. Now you are married, and her picture is still up. Well, let it remain! Why not? I know that I am still near you, that I still have a place in Charlotte's heart—the second place, but I intend to keep it. Oh, I would go mad if she could ever forget! Albert, that thought is hell! Farewell, Albert—farewell, angel from heaven—farewell, Charlotte!

March 15

I have just had an annoying experience which will drive me away from here. I am furious. It cannot be undone, and you alone are to blame; you urged and impelled me to fill a post for which I was not suited. Now I have reason to be satisfied, and so have you! But, that you may not again attribute this to my impetuous temper, I am sending you, my dear sir, a plain and simple account of the whole thing, as a chronicler of facts would record it.

Count C. likes and respects me. That is well known, and I have mentioned it to you a hundred times. Yesterday I dined with him. It was the day on which his aristocratic friends assemble at his house in the evening. I never once thought of the gathering, nor that we people of inferior rank do not belong to such society. Well, I dined with the Count; and after dinner we adjourned to the great hall. We walked up and down together; and I conversed with him, and with Colonel B., who joined us; and in this manner the hour for the assembly approached. God knows, I was unsuspecting enough, when who should enter but the honorable Lady S., accompanied by her noble husband and that nobly hatched little goose, their flat-chested and tight-laced daughter. They passed by in the traditional manner, their eyebrows raised high and their noses aristocratically turned up. As I detest the whole breed, I decided to leave, and waited only till the Count had disengaged himself from their awful prattle, to take leave, when Lady B. came in. As I always feel cheered when I see her, I stayed and talked to her, leaning over the back of her chair, and did not notice till a little later that she seemed uneasy and answered me in an embarrassed manner. I was struck by this. "Heavens!" I said to myself, "is she like the rest of them?" I felt irritated and was about to withdraw; but I remained, making excuses for her conduct, imagining that she did not mean it, and still hoping to receive some friendly recognition. The rest of the company now arrived. There was Baron F. in a complete wardrobe that dated from the coronation of Francis I; the Chancellor N. (here called—*in qualitate*—von N.) with his deaf wife; the shabbily dressed J., whose old-fashioned coat bore evidence of some modernization—all these people were coming in. I talked with some of my acquaintances, but they answered me curtly. I was preoccupied with Lady B., and did not notice that the women at the end of the room were whispering, that the murmur extended by degrees to the men, that Lady S. talked to the Count (this was all later related to me by Lady B.); till at length the Count came up to me and took me to the window. "You know our curious customs," he said. "I gather the company is a little displeased at your presence. I would not on any account wish to . . ." "I beg Your Excellency's pardon!" I exclaimed. "I ought to have thought of this before, but I know you will forgive this *faux pas*. I meant to leave," I added, "some time ago, but my evil genius detained me." I smiled and bowed to take my leave. He shook me by the hand, in a manner which expressed everything. I withdrew from the illustrious assembly, sprang into a carriage, and drove to M. to watch the setting sun from the top of the hill, and read that beautiful passage in

Homer where Ulysses is entertained by the hospitable swine-herd. How delightful all that was!

I returned home to supper in the evening. Only a few persons were still in the dining room. They had turned up a corner of the tablecloth and were playing at dice. The good-natured Adelin came in, laid down his hat when he saw me, approached and said quietly, "You have had a disagreeable time." "I?" I exclaimed. "The Count made you leave the assembly." "Deuce take the assembly!" I said. "I was very glad to get some fresh air." "I am delighted," he added, "that you take it so lightly. I am only annoyed that everybody is talking about it." The whole thing began to irk me. I fancied that everyone who sat down and looked at me was thinking of this incident; and I became furious.

And now I could plunge a dagger into my heart when I hear myself pitied everywhere, and see the triumph of my enemies, who say that this is always the lot of the vain whose heads are turned with conceit, who affect to be above convention and similar nonsense.

Say what you will of independence, but show me the man who can patiently put up with the laughter of rascals when they have an advantage over him. Only when their talk is empty nonsense can he suffer it with indifference.

———◆———

March 16

Everything conspires against me. I met Lady B. today. I joined her; and when we were at a little distance from her companions, I could not help expressing my surprise at her changed manner toward me. "O Werther!" she said warmly. "You who know my heart, how could you so mistake my distress? How I suffered for you from the moment you entered the room! I saw it coming; a hundred times I was on the point of mentioning it to you. I knew that the S.'s and T.'s with their husbands, would leave the room rather than remain in your company. I knew that the Count would not break with them: and now all this excitement!" "How do you mean?" I exclaimed, and tried to conceal my emotion; for all that Adelin had mentioned to me yesterday suddenly came back to me. "Oh, how much it has already cost me!" said this enchanting girl, her eyes filled with tears. I could scarcely control myself, and was ready to throw myself at her feet. "What do you mean?" I cried. Tears ran down her cheeks. She wiped them away without attempting to conceal them. "You know my aunt," she continued; "she was present: and you can imagine what she thought of the whole affair! Last night, and this morning, Werther, I had to listen to a lecture on my acquaintance with you. I had to hear you condemned and disparaged; and I could not—I dared not—say much in your defense."

Every word she uttered was a dagger in my heart. She did not feel that it would have been merciful of her to conceal everything from me. She told me all the gossip that would be further spread, and how the malicious would triumph; how they would rejoice over the punishment of my pride, over my humiliation for that want of esteem for others with which I had often been reproached. To hear all this, Wilhelm, in a tone of the most sincere sympathy, awakened all my anger; and I am still extremely disturbed. I wish I could find someone who dared to jeer at me about all this. I would run a sword through him. The sight of his blood would be a relief. A hundred times have I seized a knife to give ease to this oppressed heart. I have heard of a noble race of horses that instinctively bite open a vein when they are hot and exhausted by a long run, in order to breathe more freely. I am often tempted to open a vein, to gain everlasting liberty for myself.

I have tendered my resignation to the Court. I hope it will be accepted, and you will forgive me for not having previously consulted you. I must leave this place. I know you will all urge me to stay, and therefore—do sweeten this news to my mother. I cannot do anything for myself: how, then, should I be able to assist others? It will hurt her that I should have interrupted that career which would have made me a privy councilor, and then minister. Now I shall look behind me, instead of advancing. Argue as you will, combine all the reasons which might have induced or compelled me to remain—I am leaving; that is enough. But, that you may know where I am going, I will tell you that Prince * * *, who has been much pleased with my company, has heard of my intention to resign and has invited me to his country house to pass the spring months with him. I shall be left completely to myself; and as we agree on a good many subjects, I shall try my luck and accompany him.

For Your Information: April 19

Thanks for both your letters. I delayed my reply, and withheld this letter, till I had an answer from the Court. I feared my mother might apply to the minister to defeat my purpose. But my request is granted, my resignation is accepted. I shall not tell you with what reluctance it was accorded, or what the minister wrote; you would only renew your lamentations. The Prince has sent me a present of five and twenty ducats, with a few words that have moved me to tears. Now I shall not need the money from my mother, for which I wrote the other day.

I leave here tomorrow; and as my birthplace is only six miles away, I intend to visit it again and recall the old, happy days of my childhood. I shall enter at the same gate through which I left with my mother, when, after my father's death, she moved away from that delightful retreat to bury herself in that melancholy town of hers. Adieu, Wilhelm; you shall hear soon of my doings.

I have paid my visit to my native place with the devotion of a pilgrim, and have experienced many unexpected emotions. Near the great linden tree, a quarter of an hour from the town, I got out of the carriage and sent it on ahead so that I might enjoy the pleasure of recollection more vividly and to my heart's content. There I stood, under that same linden tree which used to be the goal and end of my walks. How things have changed! Then, in happy ignorance, I sighed for a world I did not know, where I hoped to find the stimulus and enjoyment which my heart could desire; and now, on my return from that wide world, O my friend, how many disappointed hopes and unfulfilled plans have I brought back!

As I saw the mountains which lay stretched out before me, I thought how often they had been the object of my dearest desires. Here I used to sit for hours, wishing to be there, wishing that I might lose myself in the woods and valleys that now lay so enchanting and mysterious before me—and when I had to return to town at a definite time, how unwillingly did I leave this familiar place! I approached the town; and recognized all the well-known old summerhouses; I disliked the new ones, and all the changes which had taken place. I entered the gate, and all the old feelings returned. I cannot, dear friend, go into details, charming as they were; they would be dull reading. I had intended to lodge in the market place, near our old house. As I approached, I noticed that the school in which, as children, we had been taught by that good old lady, was converted into a shop. I called to mind the restlessness, the heaviness, the tears, and heartaches which I experienced in that confinement. Every step produced some particular impression. No pilgrim in the Holy Land could meet so many spots charged with pious memories, and his soul can hardly be moved with greater devotion. One incident will serve for illustration. I followed the stream down to a farm—it used to be a favorite walk of mine—and I paused where we boys used to amuse ourselves making ducks and drakes upon the water. I remember so well how I sometimes watched the course of that same stream, following it with strange feelings, and romantic ideas of the countries it was to pass through; but my imagination was soon exhausted. Yet I knew that the water continued flowing on and on . . . and I lost myself completely in the contemplation of the infinite distance. Exactly like this, my friend, so happy and so rich were the thoughts of the ancients. Their feelings and their poetry were fresh as childhood. And when Ulysses talks of the immeasurable sea and boundless earth, his words are true, natural, deeply felt, and mysterious. Of what use is it that I have learned, with every schoolboy, that the world is round? Man needs but little earth for his happiness, and still less for his final rest.

I am at present at the Prince's hunting lodge. He is a man with whom one can live quite well. He is honest and simple. There are, however, some curious characters about him whom I cannot quite understand. They are not dishonest, and yet they do not seem thoroughly honorable men. Sometimes I am disposed to trust them, and yet I cannot persuade myself to confide in them. It annoys me to hear the Prince talk of things which he has only read or heard of, and always from the point of view from which they have been represented by others.

He values my understanding and talents more highly than my heart, but I am proud of my heart alone. It is the sole source of everything—all our strength, happiness, and misery. All the knowledge I possess everyone else can acquire, but my heart is all my own.

May 25

I have a plan in my head of which I did not want to speak to you until it was accomplished; but now that it has not materialized, I may as well mention it. I wished to enter the army, and had long been thinking about it. This was the chief reason for my coming here with the Prince, who is a general in the * * * service. I mentioned my intention to him during one of our walks together; but he dissuaded me, and I should have had to be really anxious about it, and not merely playing with the idea to disregard his reasons.

June 11

Say what you will, I can't stay any longer. Why should I? Time hangs heavy on my hands. The Prince is as gracious to me as anyone could be, and yet I am not at my ease. There is, at any rate, little in common between us. He is a man of understanding, but quite of the ordinary kind. His conversation affords me no more amusement than I should derive from any well-written book. I shall remain a week longer, and then start again on my travels. My sketches are the best things I have done since I came here. The Prince has a feeling for the Arts, and would be more sensitive still if his mind were not fettered by pseudo-scientific ideas and commonplace terminology; I often lose patience when, with glowing imagination, I express my feelings of Art and Nature, and he, thinking to be especially understanding, spoils everything with his clichés.

June 16

I am a wanderer only, a pilgrim, through the world. But what more are you?

June 18

Where am I going? I will tell you in confidence. I must stay here a fortnight longer, and then I had a notion to visit the mines in * * *. But I am only deluding myself. The fact is, I want to be near Charlotte again, that is all. I smile at my own heart, and must obey it.

July 29

No! it is well as it is—all is well! I—her husband! Oh God, Who gave me my life, if Thou hadst destined this happiness for me, my whole life would have been one continued prayer of thanks!

I will not complain—forgive these tears, forgive these vain wishes. She—my wife! To have held that dearest of Heaven's creatures in my arms! My whole body shakes, Wilhelm, when Albert embraces her slender waist!

And shall I confess it? Why not, Wilhelm? She would have been happier with me than with him. Albert is not the man to satisfy the wishes of such a heart. He lacks a certain sensibility; he lacks—put it any way you like—their hearts do not beat in unison. At a passage in some beloved book, when my heart and Charlotte's seem to meet, and in a hundred other instances when our feelings are revealed by the story of some other character . . . But, dear Wilhelm, he loves her with all his heart; and such a love is worth a great deal.

I have been interrupted by an insufferable visitor. I have dried my tears; my thoughts are elsewhere. Adieu, my dear friend!

August 4

I am not alone in my unhappiness. All men are disappointed in their hopes and deceived in their expectations. I visited that good woman under the linden. The eldest boy ran out to meet me; his shouts of joy brought out his mother, who looked downcast. Her first words were: "Alas! dear sir, my little Hans is dead." He was the youngest of her children. I was silent. "And my husband has returned from Switzerland empty-handed; and if some kind people had not helped him, he would have had to beg his way home. He was taken ill with fever on his journey." I could say nothing, but gave something to the little one. She offered me some fruit, which I accepted, and left the place with a heavy heart.

I change at the turn of the hand. Sometimes a happy prospect seems to open before me; but alas! it is only for a moment; and then, when I am lost in dreams, I cannot help saying to myself, "What if Albert were to die?—Yes, she would become—and I should be"—and so I pursue a chimera, till it leads me to the edge of a precipice before which I shudder.

When I leave through the same town gate, and walk along the same road which first took me to Charlotte, how different it all used to be! All, all is changed! No trace of that past world, no throb of my heart is the same. I feel like the ghost that has returned to the burnt-out castle which it had built in more splendid times, adorned with costly magnificence, and left lavishly furnished, on its death bed to a beloved son.

I sometimes cannot understand how another can love her so, dare love her, when I love nothing in this world so completely, so devotedly, as I love her, when I know only her, and have nothing but her in the whole world.

Yes, so it is! As Nature turns to autumn, it becomes autumn within me and around me. My leaves are sear and yellow, and the trees near by are divested of their leaves. Do you remember my writing to you about a peasant lad shortly after my arrival here? I inquired again about him in Wahlheim. They say he had been dismissed from his service, and nobody wanted to have anything to do with him. I met him yesterday on the road, going to a neighboring village. I spoke to him, and he told me his story. It touched me immensely, as you will easily understand when I repeat it to you. But why trouble you? Why not keep my anguish and sorrow to myself? Why distress you and give you a chance to pity and blame me? No matter; this, too, is part of my destiny.

At first the lad answered my inquiries with a sort of subdued melancholy, which seemed more shyness than anything else; but as he began to recognize me, he spoke with less reserve, and openly admitted his faults and deplored his misfortune. I wish, dear friend, I could give true expression to his language. He confessed, in fact he told me, with a sort of pleasurable recollection, that after my departure his passion for that woman grew daily, until at last he knew neither what he did nor what he said, nor what was to become of him. He could neither eat nor drink nor sleep; he felt suffocated; he did what he was not supposed to do, and forgot all orders; he seemed haunted by an evil spirit, till one day, knowing that the woman had gone upstairs, he had followed, or rather, been drawn after her. She would not listen to him, and he had used violence. He does not know what happened; but he called God to witness that his intentions had always been honest, and that he wanted nothing more sincerely than that they should get married and spend their lives together. After he had talked for awhile, he began to hesitate, as if there were something which he had not the courage to utter, till at length he admitted with some confusion that she had encouraged him now and again and had allowed him liberties. He broke off two or three times in his story, and assured me most earnestly that he had no wish to make her bad, as he put it; he loved her as sincerely as ever; that he had never told the story before and had spoken of it to me only to prove that he was not completely worthless and mad. And here, my friend, I must start that old song which you know I repeat forever. If I could only describe the man as he stood, and stands now before me—could only convey it all to you, you would feel that I do and must sympathize with his fate. Enough; you, who know my misfortune and my disposition, can easily understand what draws me toward every unfortunate being, but particularly toward this one.

As I reread this letter, I find I have forgotten to tell you the end of my tale; it is easily supplied. She fought him off, just as her brother appeared, who had long hated him and wanted him turned out of the house because, as his sister was childless, he was afraid that a second marriage might deprive his children of the handsome fortune they expected from her. The man was dismissed at once, and such a row was made about the whole business that she dared not take him back, even if she had wanted it. She has since hired another helper, with whom, they say, her brother is equally displeased, and whom she is likely to marry; but I am told that the brother is determined not to tolerate it.

This story is neither exaggerated nor embellished; as a matter of fact, I have told it very, very feebly, and the conventional moral phrases that I have used may make it cruder than it should be.

This love, this constancy, this passion, is no poetical fiction. It is real, and exists in its greatest purity amongst that class of people whom we call rude, uneducated; we—the would-be educated—who are so civilized that we are nothing. Read this story with respect, I beg of you. I am quiet today, as I write this; you see by my handwriting that I am not so excited as usual. Read this account, Wilhelm, and imagine that it might well be the story of your friend! Yes, it has happened to me; it will happen to me; and I am not half so brave, not half so determined as that poor wretch with whom I hardly dare to compare myself.

September 5

She had written a letter to her husband in the country, where
he had official business. It began, "My dearest love, come back
as soon as you can; I await you with all my love." A friend who
came to the house brought word that, for certain reasons,
Albert would not return immediately. The letter was not sent,
and the same evening it fell into my hands. I read it, and smiled.
She asked me for the reason. "What a heavenly gift is imagination!" I exclaimed; "for a moment I thought that this was
written to me." She changed the subject and seemed displeased.
I was silent.

September 6

It cost me a great deal to part with that plain blue coat I wore
the first time I danced with Charlotte. But I could not possibly
wear it any longer. I have ordered a new one, exactly like the
other, even to the collar and facings, and a new waistcoat and a
pair of breeches.

But it is not the same. I don't know why . . . . I hope in time
I shall like it better.

September 12

She has been away for a few days to meet Albert. Today I
visited her: she rose to greet me, and, overjoyed, I kissed her
hand.

A canary flew from the mirror, and settled on her shoulder. "Here is a new friend," she said and coaxed him to perch on her hand; "he is a present for the children. What a dear he is! Look at him! When I feed him, he flutters with his wings, and pecks so nicely. He can kiss me, too—look!"

She held the bird to her mouth; and he pressed her sweet lips as if he felt the bliss.

"He shall kiss you too," she added, and held the bird toward me. His little beak moved from her mouth to mine, and the touch of his peck seemed like the foretaste of the sweetest happiness.

"His kiss," I said, "is greedy; he wants food, and seems disappointed by these unsatisfactory endearments."

"He eats out of my mouth," she continued, and gave him a few morsels between her lips, smiling and happy to share her love so innocently.

I turned away. She should not do this. She should not excite my imagination with all this heavenly bliss nor awaken my heart from its slumbers to which the monotony of life sometimes lulls it. And why not? She trusts me! She knows how much I love her.

September 15

It makes me furious, Wilhelm, to think that there should be people incapable of appreciating the few things of real value in life. You remember the walnut trees at St. under which I used to sit with Charlotte at the old vicar's—those glorious trees which so often filled my heart with delight, how they adorned the parsonage yard, with their cool and wide branches! and how pleasing it was to remember the generations of pastors who planted them so many years ago! The schoolmaster has frequently mentioned the name of one of them, which he learned from his grandfather. He must have been an excellent man; and, under the shade of those old trees, his memory was ever sacred to me. With tears in his eyes the schoolmaster told us yesterday that those trees had been felled—cut down! I could kill the dog who struck the first blow. And I must put up with it! If I had only two such trees in my own yard, and one died from old age, I should weep with real grief. But there is one remarkable thing about it—the feelings of the people—the whole village is angry; and I hope the vicar's wife will soon find out, when the villagers will no longer bring her butter and eggs and other presents, how much she has wounded the feelings of the people. It was she who did it—the wife of the present minister (our good old man is dead)—a haggard, sickly creature who has, of course, every reason to disregard the world as the world completely disregards her. The silly woman affects to be learned, pretends to examine the canonical books of the Bible, lends her aid to the newfangled reformation of Christendom, moral and critical, and shrugs her shoulders at the mention of Lavater's enthusiasms. Her health is broken, and she therefore takes no pleasure in the joys of God's earth. Only that sort of creature could have cut down my walnut trees! I cannot keep calm! Listen to her reasons: the falling leaves make the yard wet and dirty; the branches obstruct the light; boys throw stones at the nuts when they are ripe and the noise affects her nerves and disturbs her profound reflections, as she weighs the merits of Kennicott, Semler, and Michaelis. When I saw that all the villagers, particularly the old people, were displeased, I asked why they allowed it. "Ah, sir!" they replied, "when the steward orders, what can we poor peasants do?" But one good thing has happened. The steward and the vicar (who for once thought to reap some advantage from his wife's whims) intended to divide the trees between them. The revenue office, being informed of it, revived an old claim to the ground where the trees had stood, and sold them to the highest bidder. There they lie!

If I were the Prince, I should know how to deal with them all—vicar, wife, steward, and revenue office. Prince, did I say? If I were the Prince I should care little about the trees that grew in my country.

Only to look into her black eyes is a source of happiness! And what grieves me is that Albert does not seem so happy as he —hoped to be—as I—thought I would be—if—I don't like to use dashes, but here I cannot express myself in any other way; and I am probably explicit enough.

October 12

Ossian has superseded Homer in my heart. What a world into which that magnificent poet carries me! To wander over the heath, blown about by the winds, which conjure up by the feeble light of the moon the spirits of our ancestors; to hear from the mountaintops, mid the roar of the rivers, their plaintive groans coming from deep caverns; and the laments of the maiden who sighs and perishes on the moss-covered, grass-grown tomb of the warrior who loved her. I meet the grey bard as he wanders on the heath seeking the footsteps of his fathers;. alas! he finds only their tombstones. Then, turning to the pale moon, as it sinks beneath the waves of the rolling sea, the memory of past ages stirs in the soul of the hero—days when the friendly light shone upon the brave warriors and their bark laden with spoils, returning in triumph. When I read the deep sorrow in his countenance, see his dying glory sink exhausted

83

into the grave, as he draws new and heart-thrilling delight from the impotent shades of his beloved ones, casting a look on the cold earth and the tall grass, exclaiming, "The traveler will come—will come who has seen my beauty, and will ask, 'Where is the bard—the illustrious son of Fingal?' He will pass over my tomb, and seek me in vain!"—O friend, I would, like a true and noble knight, draw my sword, and deliver my lord from the long and painful languor of a living death, and dismiss my own soul to follow the demigod whom my hand had set free!

October 19

Alas! the void—the fearful void within me! Sometimes I think, if I could once—only once—press her to my heart, this void would all be filled.

October 26

Yes, I feel certain, Wilhelm, and every day more certain, that the existence of any being is of very little consequence. A friend of Charlotte's came to see her just now. I withdrew to another room and took up a book; but, finding I could not read, I sat down to write. I heard them talk quietly about all sorts of things, gossip of the town: one was going to be married; another was ill, very ill—"She has a dry cough, you can see the bones in her face, and she faints occasionally. I wouldn't give a penny for her life," said the friend. "N. is in very poor health, too," said Charlotte. "His limbs begin to swell already," answered the other; and my lively imagination carried me at once to the bedside of those poor people. I saw them struggling against death, with all the agonies of pain and horror. And these ladies, Wilhelm, talked of all this with as much indifference as if they were discussing the death of a stranger. And when I look around the room where I now am—when I see Charlotte's apparel lying about, and Albert's papers, and the furniture which is so familiar to me, even to the very inkstand which I am using—when I think what I am to this family!—all in all. My friends respect me; I often make them happy, and my heart seems as if it could not beat without them; and yet—if I were to die, if I were to leave this circle—would they feel—or how long would they feel—the void which my loss would make in their lives? How long? Yes, such is the frailty of man that even where he has the greatest certainty of his own being, where he makes the truest and most forcible impression—in the memory, in the heart of his beloved, there also he must perish—vanish—and that so soon!

October 27

I could tear open my breast and dash out my brains to think how little we can actually mean to each other. No one can communicate to me those sensations of love, joy, rapture, and delight which I do not myself possess; and though my heart may be filled with bliss, I cannot make him happy who stands before me cold and indifferent.

October 27, in the evening

I possess so much, but my love for her absorbs it all. I possess so much, but without her I have nothing.

A hundred times I have been on the verge of embracing her. God! What a torture it is to see so much loveliness before us, and yet not dare to touch it! And touching with our hands is the most natural of human instincts. Do not children touch everything they see? And I?

God knows how often I lie down to sleep wishing and even hoping that I may never awaken again! And in the morning, when I open my eyes, I see the sun once more, and am wretched. If I were whimsical, I might blame the weather, or an acquaintance, or disappointment, for my discontented mind; this insupportable load of trouble would not rest entirely upon myself. But alas! I feel all too clearly that I alone am to blame for my woe. To blame? No, my own heart contains the source of all my sorrow, as it previously contained the source of all my pleasure. Am I not the same who once enjoyed an abundance of happiness, who at every step saw paradise open before him, and whose heart was ever ready to embrace the whole world? And this heart is now dead; no delight will flow from it. My eyes are dry; and my senses, no more refreshed by soft tears, wither and consume my brain. I suffer much, for I have lost the only joy of my life: that active, sacred power with which I created worlds around me—it is no more. When I look from my window at the distant hills, and behold the morning sun breaking through the mists, and illuminating the country around, which is still wrapped in silence, and the gentle stream winds among the willows, which have shed their leaves; when this magnificent scene lies there before me like a vanished picture, and all this glory cannot pump one single drop of happiness from my heart into my brain—there he stands, the poor fellow, in the face of God's glory, like a dry spring or an empty pail. I have often thrown myself to the ground and implored God for tears as the farmer prays for rain when the sky above him is brazen and the ground about him is parched.

But I feel that God does not grant sunshine or rain to our furious prayers. Those bygone days, whose memory now torments me—why were they so happy? Because I waited with patience for the blessings of His spirit and received His gifts with the grateful feelings of a thankful heart.

———————◆———————

November 8

Charlotte has reproved me for my lack of self-control—and with so much tenderness and goodness! I have been drinking a little more wine than usual. "Don't do it," she said; "think of Charlotte!" "Think of you!" I answered. "Need you tell me that? Think of you—or do not think of you! You are always before me! This morning I sat on the spot where, a few days ago, you stepped from the carriage, and—" She changed the subject to prevent me from getting deeper into it. My friend, I am lost; she can do with me what she pleases.

———————◆———————

November 15

Thank you, Wilhelm, for your kind sympathy, for your well-meaning advice; and I implore you not to be disturbed. Let me endure to the end. In spite of my weariness, I have still strength enough to see it through. I respect religion—you know I do. I feel that it can give strength to the feeble and comfort to the afflicted; but does it affect all men alike? I look at the great world: you will see thousands for whom religion has never existed, thousands for whom it will never exist, whether it be preached to them or not; must it, then, necessarily exist for me? Does not the Son of God Himself say that they are His whom the Father has given to Him? Have I been given to Him? What if our Father should want to keep me for Himself, as my heart sometimes tells me? I pray you, do not misinterpret this. Do not see mockery in these harmless words. I pour out my whole soul before you. Silence would have been better; I do not like to waste words on a subject of which everyone else knows as little as I do. What is the destiny of man but to fill up the measure of his sufferings, and to drink his allotted cup of bitterness? And if that same cup proved bitter to the Son of God, why should I affect a foolish pride and call it sweet? Why should I be ashamed of shrinking at that fearful moment when my whole being trembles between existence and annihilation; when the remembrance of the past, like a flash of lightning, illuminates the dark abyss of the future; when everything dissolves around me, and the whole world vanishes? Is it not the voice of a creature oppressed beyond all resource, insufficient, irresistibly plunging to destruction, and groaning deeply at its inadequate strength: "My God! my God! why hast Thou forsaken me?" And should I feel ashamed to utter these words? Should I not shudder at the moment which had its fears even for Him Who folds up the heavens like a garment?

November 21

She does not see, she does not feel that she is preparing a poison which will destroy us both; and I drink deeply of the draught that is to prove my destruction. What mean those looks of kindness with which she often—often? no, not often, but sometimes—looks at me, that politeness with which she hears an involuntary expression of my feeling, the tender pity for my suffering which she sometimes seems to show?

Yesterday, when I took leave, she took my hand and said, "Adieu, dear Werther." Dear Werther! It was the first time she ever called me "dear"; it went through me. I have repeated it a hundred times; and last night, as I was going to bed and talked to myself about nothing in particular, I suddenly said, "Good night, dear Werther!" and I could not help laughing at myself.

November 22

I cannot pray, "Let her be mine!" Yet she often seems to belong to me. I cannot pray. "Give her to me!" for she is another's. I try to quiet my suffering by all sorts of cool arguments. If I let myself go, I could compose a whole litany of antitheses.

November 24

She feels what I suffer. This morning her look pierced my very soul. I found her alone, and said nothing; she looked at me. I no longer saw in her face the charms of beauty or the spark of her mind; these had disappeared. But I was struck by an expression much more touching—a look of the deepest sympathy and of the gentlest pity. Why was I afraid to throw myself at her feet? Why did I not dare to take her in my arms, and answer her with a thousand kisses? She turned to her piano for relief, and in a low and sweet voice accompanied the music with delicious sounds. Her lips never appeared lovelier; they seemed but just to open, that they might drink the sweet tones which came from the instrument, and return the delicate echo from her sweet mouth. Oh, if only I could convey all this to you! I was quite overcome, and bending down, pronounced this vow: "Never will I dare to kiss you, beautiful lips which the spirits of Heaven guard." And yet I will—but it stands like a barrier before my soul—this bliss—and then die to expiate the sin! Is it sin?

———◆———

November 26

I often say to myself, "You alone are wretched; all others are happy; none are distressed like you." Then I read a passage of an ancient poet, and it is as if I looked into my own heart. I have so much to endure! Have men before me ever been so wretched?

———◆———

November 30

Never, it seems, shall I be at rest! Wherever I go, something occurs to upset me. Today—alas, for our destiny! alas, for human nature!

At noon I went to walk by the river—I had no appetite. Everything around seemed gloomy; a cold and damp west wind blew from the mountains, and heavy, grey clouds spread over the plain. I noticed at a distance a man in a shabby green coat, climbing among the rocks, and apparently looking for herbs. When I approached, he turned round at the noise; and I saw that he had an interesting face, in which a quiet melancholy, strongly marked by kindness, formed the principal feature. His long black hair was held in two coils by pins, and the rest was braided and hung down his back. As his dress indicated a person of lower rank, I thought he would not take it ill if I inquired about his business; I therefore asked what he was looking for. He replied, with a deep sigh, that he was looking for flowers and could find none. "But this is not the season," I observed, with a smile. "Oh, there are so many flowers!" he answered, as he came nearer. "In my garden there are roses and honeysuckles of two sorts: one sort was given to me by my father; they grow like weeds. I have been looking for them these two days, and cannot find them. There are flowers out there, yellow, blue, and red; and that centaury has a very pretty blossom: but I can find none of them." I suspected something strange, and asked him in a roundabout way what he intended to do with his flowers. A curious twitching smile spread over his face. Holding one finger to his mouth, he implored me not to betray him; then he told me that he had promised to gather a nosegay for his mistress. "That is a good idea," said I. "Oh!" he replied, "she has many other things as well; she is very rich." "And yet," I continued, "she likes your nosegays." "Oh, she has jewels and a crown!" he exclaimed. I asked who she was. "If the States-General would only pay me." he added, "I should be a different person. There was a time when I was well off; but that is past; now I am—" He raised his tear-filled eyes to heaven. "And you were happy once?" I asked him. "Ah, would I were so still!" was his reply. "I was as gay and contented as a man can be." An old woman, who was coming toward us, now called out:

"Henry, Henry! where are you? We have been looking for you everywhere. Come and eat." "Is that your son?" I inquired, as I went toward her. "Yes," she said; "he is my poor, unfortunate son. The Lord has sent me a heavy cross." I asked how long he had been like this. She answered: "He has been as calm as he is at present for about six months. Thank Heaven that he has so far recovered. For a whole year he was quite violent, and chained down in a madhouse. Now he harms no one, but talks of nothing but kings and emperors. He used to be a good, quiet boy, who helped support me, and wrote a very fine hand. But all at once he became melancholy, was seized with a violent fever, grew distracted, and is now as you see. If I were to tell you, sir—" I interrupted her by asking what period it was in which he said he had been so happy. "Poor boy!" she exclaimed, with a smile of compassion, "he means the time when he was completely out of his mind—a time he never stops praising—when he was in the madhouse and unaware of his condition." I was thunderstruck. I put a piece of money in her hand and hastened away.

"When you were happy!" I exclaimed, as I returned quickly to the town, "happy as a fish in water!" God in heaven! is this the destiny of man? To be happy only before he has acquired his reason and again after he has lost it? Poor fellow! And yet I envy your fate; I envy the delusion to which you are a victim. You go forth with joy to gather flowers for your queen in winter, and grieve when you can find none, and cannot understand why they do not grow. And I—I wander forth without hope, without purpose; and I return as I came. You imagine what you would be if the States-General paid you. Happy mortal, who can ascribe your wretchedness to an earthly cause! You do not know, you do not feel, that in your own distracted heart and disordered brain dwells the source of that unhappiness which all the kings on earth cannot relieve.

Let that man die unconsoled who can deride the invalid for undertaking a journey to distant, healthful springs—which may only increase his sickness and hasten his painful death—or who can exult over the despairing mind of a sinner who, to obtain peace of conscience and relief from misery, makes a pilgrimage to the Holy Sepulchre. Each laborious step which hurts his wounded feet on rough and untrodden paths is balm for his troubled soul, and the journey of many a weary day brings nightly relief to his anguished heart. Will you dare call this illusion, you pompous fools? Madness! O God! Thou seest my tears. Thou hast allotted us our portion of misery: must we also have brethren to persecute us, to deprive us of our consolation, of our trust in Thee and in Thy love and mercy? For our trust in the virtue of the healing root or in the strength of the vine—what else is it but belief in Thee, from Whom all that surrounds us derives its healing and restoring powers? Father, Whom I know not—Who wert once wont to fill my soul, but Who now hidest Thy face from me—call me back to Thee; be silent no longer! Thy silence cannot sustain a soul which thirsts after Thee. What man, what father, could be angry with a son for returning to him unexpectedly, for falling on his neck, and exclaiming, "Here I am again, my father! Forgive me if I have shortened my journey to return before the appointed time! The world is everywhere the same—for labor and pain, pleasure and reward; but what does it all avail? I am happy only where thou art, and in thy presence I am content to suffer or enjoy." And Thou, Heavenly Father, wouldst Thou turn such a child from Thee?

December 1

Wilhelm! The man about whom I wrote to you—that man so happy in his misfortunes—was a clerk in the service of Charlotte's father; and an unhappy passion for her, which he cherished, concealed, and eventually revealed, made him lose his position. This caused his madness. Think, as you read these dry words, what an impression all this has made on me! Albert told it as calmly as you will probably read it.

———◆———

I implore you. It is all over with me. I cannot bear it any longer. Today I sat by Charlotte. She was playing on her piano all sorts of melodies, with such expression! Her little sister sat on my lap dressing her doll. Tears came into my eyes. I leaned down, and saw Charlotte's wedding ring; my tears fell—and as if by chance she began to play that favorite tune, that sweet air which has so often enchanted me. I felt comfort from a recollection of the past, of those bygone days when I heard that melody; and then I recalled all the sorrows and the disappointments which I had since endured—and then—I walked up and down the room, my heart choked with painful emotions. Finally, starting toward her with an impatient outburst, I said, "For Heaven's sake, stop it!" She stopped playing, and looked at me. Then she said, with a smile which went deep to my heart: "Werther, you are ill; your dearest food is distasteful to you. Go, I ask you, and try to calm yourself." I tore myself away. God, Thou seest my torments, and wilt end them!

———◆———

December 6

How her image haunts me! Waking or asleep, she fills all my thoughts! When I close my eyes, here, in my brain, where all the energies of inward vision are concentrated, are her black eyes. Here—I cannot express it; but if I shut my eyes, there are hers: dark as the ocean, as an abyss they lie before me, and fill the nerves of my brain.

What is man—that much praised demigod? Do not his powers fail when he most requires their use? And whether he soar in joy or sink in sorrow, is he not inevitably arrested? And whilst he fondly dreams that he is grasping at infinity, is he not at that moment made doubly aware of the dull monotony of his existence?

The Editor to the Reader

I wish that we had so many documents by his own hand about our friend's memorable last days that I did not need to interrupt the sequence of his letters by a connecting narrative.

I have felt it my duty to collect accurate information from persons well acquainted with his history. The story is simple; and all accounts agree, except for some unimportant particulars. Only with respect to the character of the persons involved do opinions and judgments vary.

All that is left to do, then, is to relate conscientiously the facts which our persistent labor has enabled us to collect, to give the letters found after his death, and to pay attention to even the slightest fragment from his pen, especially since it is so difficult to discover the true and innermost motives of men who are not of the common run.

Sorrow and discontent had taken deep root in Werther's soul, and gradually penetrated his whole being. His mind became completely deranged; perpetual excitement and mental irritation, which weakened his natural powers, produced the saddest effects upon him, and rendered him at length the victim of a weariness against which he struggled with even greater effort than he had displayed in his other misfortunes. The anguish of his heart consumed his good qualities, his vivaciousness and his keen mind; he was soon a gloomy companion—increasingly unhappy, and the more unjust in his ideas, the more wretched he became. This, at least is, the opinion of Albert's friends. They insist that Werther had been unable to appreciate so steady and simple a man as Albert, who was about to find that happiness which he had so long wished for, and who meant to make sure that he would guard this happiness for the years to come. Werther could not understand such an attitude since he himself was inclined to squander his own substance every day, only to suffer privation and distress. Albert, they said, had, in the meantime, not changed at all; he was still the man whom Werther had known, honored, and respected from the beginning. His love for Charlotte was unbounded; he was proud of her, and wanted her recognized by everyone as the noblest of human beings. Was he to blame for wishing to keep from her every appearance of suspicion? Or for his unwillingness to share this precious love with another, even for a moment, and however innocently? His friends admit that Albert frequently retired from his wife's rooms during Werther's visits; that he did so not from hatred or dislike for his friend, but rather from a feeling that his presence was oppressive to Werther.

Charlotte's father, who was confined to the house by indisposition, had sent his carriage for her, and she went out to him. It was a beautiful winter day, the first snow had fallen and covered the country.

The next morning, Werther followed Charlotte, in order that, if Albert could not meet her, he might accompany her home.

The clear weather had but little effect on his troubled mind. A heavy weight lay upon his soul, deep melancholy had taken possession of him, and his mind knew no change save from one painful thought to another.

As he was not at peace with himself, the condition of his fellow creatures was for him a perpetual source of concern and distress. He believed he had disturbed the happiness of Albert and his wife, and although he censured himself severely for this, he could not quite suppress a certain feeling of dislike for Albert.

On his way to Lotte, his thoughts dwelt on this subject. "Yes, yes," he said to himself, gnashing his teeth, "all this intimate, warm, tender and sympathetic love, this calm and lasting fidelity! What is it in reality but surfeit and indifference? Is he not infinitely more interested in any one of his miserable official duties than in his dear and incomparable wife? Does he appreciate his good fortune? Does he respect her as she deserves? He possesses her; very well—he possesses her; I know it—I have become accustomed to that thought, although it will drive me mad yet, it will kill me! And has his friend-ship for me really stood the test? Does he not regard my attachment to Charlotte as an infringement on his rights, and my attentions to her as a silent rebuke for himself? I know it perfectly well, I feel it, that he dislikes me, that he wants me to go, that my presence is irksome to him."

He would often pause suddenly and stand still as if in doubt, and seem about to turn back; but he went on, and finally, engaged in such thoughts and soliloquies, somehow against his will, he reached the hunting lodge.

He entered, and, inquiring for Charlotte and her father, he noticed that the household was in a state of considerable confusion.

The eldest boy told him that an accident had occurred at Wahlheim, that a peasant had been murdered. This made little impression upon him. Entering the room he found Charlotte pleading with her father who, in spite of his ill-ness, insisted on going to the scene of the crime in order to conduct an inquiry. The criminal was as yet unknown; the victim had been found dead at his own door that morning. Suspicions were aroused: the murdered man had been in the service of a widow, and the fellow who had previously held the job had been dismissed by her.

As soon as Werther heard this he cried excitedly: "Is it possible! I must go over there at once! I cannot stay a moment!" He hastened towards Wahlheim. He recalled the earlier meeting and did not doubt that the murderer was the man with whom he had so often spoken, and for whom he entertained so much regard. His way took him past the linden trees to the house where the body had been carried. He felt a sudden horror at the sight of the spot that he remembered so fondly. The threshold where the neighbors' children had so often played together was stained with blood. Love and attachment, the noblest feelings of human nature, had been turned to violence and murder. The huge trees stood there, leafless and covered with hoarfrost; the beautiful hedgerows which had overgrown the low wall of the churchyard were bare, and here and there, half covered with snow, gravestones were visible.

As he came nearer the inn, in front of which the whole village was assembled, he suddenly heard shouts. A troop of armed peasants approached and everyone exclaimed that the criminal had been apprehended. Werther looked, and saw at once that it was the young man who had been so attached to the widow, and whom he had sometimes met prowling about with suppressed anger and ill-concealed despair.

"What have you done?" said Werther as he approached the prisoner. The young man turned his eyes upon him in silence, and then replied with perfect composure, "No one will marry her now, and she will marry no one." The prisoner was taken into the inn, and Werther left.

His mind was much excited by this terrible incident. For one moment he was lifted out of his usual feelings of melancholy, moroseness, and indifference to everything around him. He was seized by pity for the prisoner, and felt an indescribable urge to save him from his impending fate. He felt for the man, thought his crime quite excusable, and identified himself so completely with the fellow that he was convinced he could make everyone view the matter in the light in which he saw it himself. He wanted to defend him, and began composing an eloquent speech for the occasion; and on his way to the hunting lodge he could not help uttering aloud all the things which he resolved to put before the judge.

On his arrival, he found Albert, and was a little perplexed by this meeting. But he soon recovered himself, and with much warmth expressed his sympathy to the judge. The latter shook his head doubtingly; and although Werther urged his case with the utmost zeal, feeling, and determination, yet, as can be easily supposed, the judge was not much impressed by his appeal. On the contrary, he interrupted him, reasoned seriously with him, and even rebuked him for being the advocate of a murderer. He demonstrated that, if Werther were right, every law would be violated, and the public security utterly destroyed. He added that he could himself do nothing, without assuming the greatest responsibility; that everything must proceed in due course, and go through the regular channels.

Werther, however, did not give in, and even suggested to the judge to connive at the flight of the prisoner. But this proposal was, of course, rejected. Albert, who eventually took part in the discussion, agreed with the judge. At this Werther became enraged, and took his leave in great anger, after the judge had repeatedly said "No, he cannot be saved." How deeply these words must have struck him can be seen from a slip of paper which was found among his belongings, and which was undoubtedly written on that same day.

"You cannot be saved, unfortunate man! I see only too well that we cannot be saved!"

Werther was highly irritated at the remarks which Albert had made to the judge in this matter of the prisoner. He thought he could detect in them a little bitterness towards himself personally; and although, upon reflection, it could not escape his sound judgment that their view of the matter was correct, he felt the greatest possible reluctance to make such an admission.

A note of Werther's upon this point, expressive of his general feelings towards Albert, was found among his papers.

"What is the use of continually repeating to myself that he is a good and admirable man? It tears my heart, and I cannot be just towards him."

On the same evening, the weather was mild, and Charlotte and Albert walked home together. From time to time, she looked about her, as if she missed Werther's company. Albert began to speak of him, and criticized him, though most fairly. He alluded to his unfortunate attachment, and wished it were possible to send him away, "I should like it for our sake," he added; "and I would ask you to do what you can to alter his behavior towards you, and to visit you less frequently. The world is full of gossip, and I know that here and there people are talking about us." Charlotte made no reply, and Albert seemed to feel what her silence meant. At least from that time on he never spoke of Werther again; and when she brought up the subject, he allowed the conversation to die, or else he changed the subject.

The vain attempt Werther made to save the unhappy murderer was the last feeble glimmering of a flame about to be extinguished. He sank only more deeply into a state of gloom and inactivity, and was nearly brought to distraction when he learned that he might be summoned as a witness against the prisoner, who now denied everything.

His mind became oppressed by the recollection of every misfortune in his past life. The annoyance he had suffered at the ambassador's, and his subsequent failures and troubles were revived in his memory. All this, he felt, gave him a right to be inactive. Without any energy left he seemed cut off from every pursuit and occupation which makes the business of everyday life. He became a victim to his own susceptibility, and to his restless passion for the most enchanting and beloved of women, whose peace he destroyed. In this unvarying monotony of existence his days were consumed; and his powers became exhausted since he lived without purpose or design, until he seemed ever nearer his sorrowful end.

A few letters which he left behind, and which we here subjoin, afford the best proof of his anguish of mind and of the depth of his passion, as well as of his doubts and struggles, and of his weariness of life.

———◆———

"December 12

Dear Wilhelm, I am reduced to the state of mind of those unfortunate creatures who believe they are pursued by an evil spirit. Sometimes I am oppressed, not by apprehension or fear, but by an inexpressible inner fury which seems to tear up my heart and choke me. Then I wander about amid the horrors of the night, at this dreadful time of year.

Yesterday evening it drove me outside. A rapid thaw had suddenly set in: I had been told that the river had risen, that the brooks had all overflowed their banks, and that the whole valley of Wahlheim was under water! I rushed out after eleven o'clock. I beheld a terrible sight. The furious torrents rolled from the mountains in the moonlight—fields, trees, and hedges were torn up, and the entire valley was one deep lake, agitated by the roaring wind! And when the moon shone forth, and tinged the black clouds, and the wild torrent at my feet foamed and resounded with awful and grand impetuosity, I was overcome by feelings of fear and delight at once. With arms extended, I looked down into the yawning abyss, and cried, "Down! Down!" For a moment I was lost in the intense delight of ending my sorrows and my sufferings by a plunge into that gulf! But then I felt as if rooted to the earth, and incapable of ending my woes! My hour is not yet come: I feel it is not. Oh, Wilhelm, how willingly would I have given up my human existence to merge with the wind, or to embrace the torrent! Will not some day this imprisoned soul be released for such bliss?

I turned with sadness toward a favorite spot beneath a willow where I used to sit with Charlotte after a long walk. It, too, was submerged and I could hardly make out the willow tree. Wilhelm! And her meadows, I thought, the country near her lodge, the arbor devastated by the floods . . . And a ray of past happiness fell upon me, as the mind of a prisoner is cheered by a dream of flocks, and fields and bygone honors. But I stood firm!—I have the courage to die! Perhaps I should have—but here I now sit, like an old woman who gathers her own firewood and begs her bread from door to door to ease her joyless, waning life, and lengthen it by a few moments."

◆

"December 14

What is the matter with me, Wilhelm? I am afraid of myself! Is not my love for her the purest, most holy and most brotherly? Have I ever felt a single reprehensible desire? But I will make no protestations. And now—dreams! How right were the people who ascribed all these conflicting feelings to some strange supernatural power! Last night—I tremble as I say it—I held her in my arms. I pressed her to me and covered with countless kisses those dear lips of hers which murmered in response words of love. Our eyes were one in the bliss of ecstasy. God—am I wrong still to feel that happiness, to recall once more those rapturous moments with the deepest delight? Charlotte! Charlotte! I am lost! My senses are confused, for a week now I have been almost beside myself. My eyes are filled with tears—nowhere at ease, yet everywhere at home—I wish for nothing—I have no desires —better I were gone."

———◆———

Under the circumstances narrated above, a determination to quit this world had now taken fixed possession of Werther's mind. Since his return to Charlotte, this thought had been the object of all his hopes and wishes; it was to be no precipitate, rash act; he would proceed with calmness and with the most perfect deliberation.

His troubles and inner struggles may be seen from the following note, which was found, without date, amongst his papers, and seems to be the beginning of a letter to Wilhelm:

"Her presence, her fate, her sympathy with mine, press the last tears from my withered brain.

To lift the curtain, to step behind it—that is all! And why all these doubts and delays? Because we know not what it is like behind—because there is no return—and because our mind suspects that all is darkness and confusion, where we have no certainty."

Eventually the melancholy thought of death became more and more familiar to him; and his resolution was now final and irrevocable, the following ambiguous letter addressed to his friend may afford some proof of it:

I am grateful to you, Wilhelm, for having so well understood what I said. Yes, you are right: it is better that I should go. Your suggestion that I should return to you does not quite please me; at least, I should like to make a little excursion on the way, particularly as we may now expect the frost to last, and the roads to be good. I am delighted that you will come to fetch me; only postpone it for a fortnight, and await another letter from me. One should not pluck the fruit before it is ripe, and a fortnight sooner or later makes a great difference. Ask my mother to pray for her son, and tell her to forgive me for all the unhappiness I have caused her. It has ever been my fate to sadden those to whom I owed happiness. Adieu, my dearest friend. May every blessing of heaven be upon you. Farewell."

We hardly dare to express in words the emotions with which Charlotte's soul was filled during the whole of this time, both in relation to her husband and to her unfortunate friend. But, knowing her character, we may form some idea of her frame of mind; a perceptive feminine reader may be able to fathom her soul and feel with her.

It is certain that she was determined to keep Werther at a distance; and if she hesitated, it was only from a sincere feeling of pity, knowing what it would cost him—indeed that he would find it almost impossible to comply with her wishes. But for various reasons she felt at that time more inclined to be firm. Her husband kept silent about the whole matter, as she herself had never made it a subject of conversation. But she felt all the more bound to prove to him by her conduct that her views agreed with his.

On the same day—it was the Sunday before Christmas—on which Werther had written the last-mentioned letter to his friend, he came in the evening to Charlotte's house and found her alone. She was busy arranging some toys for her brothers and sisters which were to be distributed to them on Christmas Day. He talked of the pleasure of the children, and about those times when the unexpected opening of the door and the appearance of the Christmas tree, decorated with fruit and candy, and lighted up with wax candles, causes such paradisical joy. "You shall have a present, too, a little roll of wax tapers, and something else, if you behave well," said Charlotte, concealing her embarrassment under a sweet smile. "And what do you call behaving well? What am I to do, what can I do, dearest Charlotte?" said he. "Thursday night," she answered, "is Chistmas Eve. The children are all to be here, and my father, too. There will be a present for each; you must come too, but not before that time." Werther was taken aback. "I beg of you; it has to be," she continued. "I beg you, for my own peace of mind. We cannot go on like this any longer." He turned away from her, walked hastily up and down the room, muttering, "We cannot go on like this any longer!" Charlotte, seeing the violent state into which these words had thrown him, tried to divert his thoughts by all sorts of questions, but in vain. "No, Charlotte!" he exclaimed; "I will never see you again!" "Why?" she answered. "Werther, you can, you must see us again; only control yourself. Oh! why were you born with that excessive, that ungovernable passion for everything that is dear to you?" Then, taking his hand, she said: "I beg of you, be more calm; your talents, your understanding, your knowledge, will furnish you with a thousand delights. Be a man, and conquer this unhappy attachment towards a person who can do nothing but pity you." He gritted his teeth and looked at her gloomily. She held his hand. "Only one moment of clear thinking, Werther," she said. "Do you not see that you are deceiving yourself, that you are seeking your own destruction? Why must you love me, me only, who belong to another? I fear, I fear, that it is only the impossibility of possessing me that makes your desire for me so strong." He drew back his hand, with a fixed, angry look in his eyes, and cried, "Wise, very wise. Did Albert furnish you with this idea? It is politic, very clever." "Anyone might say it," she answered. "Is there not a woman in the whole world who could make you happy? Bring yourself to look for her, I would swear that you will find her. I have long feared for you, and for us all: you have confined yourself to us for too long. Make an effort: a short journey will distract you. Seek and find an object worthy of your love; then return and let us enjoy together the happiness of a most perfect friendship."

"This speech," replied Werther, with a cold smile, "this speech ought to be printed, for the benefit of all teachers. My dear Charlotte, allow me but a little rest, and all will be well." "But, Werther," she added, "do not come again before Christmas Eve." He was about to make some answer when Albert came in. They greeted each other coolly, and with mutual embarrassment paced up and down the room. Werther made some casual remarks; Albert did the same, and their conversation soon dropped. Albert asked his wife about one or two household matters; and, finding that they had not been done, he used some expressions which, to Werther's ear, sounded harsh. He wished to go, but could not; and remained till eight o'clock, his uneasiness and dissatisfaction continually increasing. At length, the table was laid for supper, and he took his hat and stick. Albert asked him to stay; but Werther, suspecting a polite gesture, thanked him curtly and left.

Werther returned home, took the candle from his servant,

and retired to his room alone. He talked to himself for some time, wept aloud, walked excitedly up and down his room finally, without undressing, he threw himself on the bed, where he was found by his servant at eleven o'clock, when the latter ventured to enter his room and asked whether he might take off his master's boots. Werther let him do it, but ordered him not to come in the morning till he was called.

On Monday morning, the 21st of December, he wrote the following letter to Charlotte, which was found, sealed, on his desk after his death, and was given to her. I shall insert it in sections; as it appears, from several circumstances, to have been written in that manner.

———◆———

"My mind is made up, Charlotte: I am resolved to die! I am writing you this without any romantic sentimentality, on this morning of the day when I am to see you for the last time. When you read this, my dearest, the cool grave will cover the stiff remains of that restless and unhappy man who, in the last moments of his life, knows no greater bliss than to converse with you! I have passed a dreadful night—or rather, a propitious one; for it has given me resolution, it has fixed my purpose. I am resolved to die. When I tore myself away from you yesterday, my senses were in tumult and disorder; my heart was oppressed, hope and pleasure had fled from me forever, and a cold horror had seized me. I could scarcely reach my room. I threw myself on my knees, and God, for the last time, granted me the bitter consolation of tears. A thousand ideas, a thousand schemes, raced through my mind, till at last, one fixed, final thought took possession of my heart. I intend to die. I lay down; and in the morning, in the quiet hour of awakening, I felt the same determination. I intend to die! It is not despair, but the certainty that I have reached the end, and must sacrifice myself for you. Yes, Charlotte, why should I not say it? One of us three must go: it shall be Werther. O Beloved! this heart, excited by rage and fury, has often had the monstrous impulse to murder your husband—you—myself! Now, it is decided. And in the bright, quiet evenings of summer, when you wander toward the mountains, let your thoughts turn to me; recollect how often you have watched me coming to meet you from the valley; then, look toward the churchyard to my grave, and, by the light of the setting sun, mark how the evening breeze waves the tall grass which grows above my tomb. I was calm when I began this, but now, when I see it all so vividly, I am weeping like a child."

———◆———

About ten in the morning, Werther called his servant, and, as he was dressing, told him that in a few days he intended to go away, and bade him therefore take out his clothes and prepare them for packing, call in all his accounts, fetch home the books he had lent, and give a two months' advance to some poor people to whom he usually gave a weekly allowance.

He had his meal in his room, and then mounted his horse, and went to visit the judge, who, however, was not at home. He walked pensively in the garden, and seemed anxious to bury himself in melancholy memories.

The children did not let him alone for long. They followed him, skipping and dancing, and told him that after tomorrow —and another day—and one day more, they were to receive their Christmas presents from Charlotte; and they recounted all the wonders of their imagination. "Tomorrow—and again tomorrow," said he, "and one day more!" And he kissed them tenderly. He was about to go; but the younger boy stopped him, to whisper something in his ear. He told him that his elder brothers had written beautiful New Year's wishes—so big—one for Papa, and another for Albert and Charlotte, and one for Werther; and they were to be presented early in the morning, on New Year's Day. This quite overcame him. He made each of the children a present, mounted his horse, left his regards for Papa, and rode away with tears in his eyes.

He returned home towards five o'clock and ordered the maid to keep up his fire; he told his servant to pack his books and linen in the trunk downstairs, and to sew his clothes up in a bundle. Then he probably wrote the following passage in his last letter to Charlotte:

———◆———

"You do not expect me. You think I will obey you, and not visit you again till Christmas Eve. Oh, Charlotte, today or never again! On Christmas Eve you will hold this letter in your hand; you will tremble, and moisten it with your tears. I will, I must! Oh, how glad I am that I have made up my mind!"

———◆———

In the meantime, Charlotte was in a strange mood. After her last conversation with Werther, she realized how hard it would be to part from him, and how he would suffer if he had to go.

She had, in conversation with Albert, casually mentioned that Werther would not return before Christmas Eve; and soon afterwards Albert went on horseback to see an official in the neighborhood with whom he had to transact some business that would detain him all night.

Charlotte was sitting alone. None of her family were near and her thoughts turned to her own situation: she was married to the man whose love and fidelity she trusted, to whom she was deeply devoted and who, with his steadiness and honesty seemed heaven-sent to ensure her happiness. She knew what he would always be to her and the children. On the other hand, she had grown so fond of Werther; from the very first hour of their acquaintance she had felt the sympathy between them, and their long association and many common experiences had made an indelible impression upon her heart. She had become accustomed to sharing with him every thought and feeling, and his departure threatened to create a void in her life which it would be impossible to fill. How she wished that she might change him into her brother, that she could induce him to marry one of her own friends, and that she could re-establish his friendship with Albert.

In her mind she passed all her intimate friends in review, but found something objectionable in each, and could decide upon none to whom she would consent to give him.

Amid all these reflections she felt, for the first time, deeply though half unconsciously, that it was her secret wish to keep him for herself. But she realized that she could and must not do so. Her own heart, usually so clear and light and always able to find a way out of trouble, was oppressed with a load of distress that seemed to bar any prospect of happiness. She was depressed, and a dark cloud obscured her vision.

It was half past six, when she heard Werther's step on the stairs. She recognized his voice, as he enquired if she were at home. Her heart beat furiously—we might almost say, for the first time—at his arrival. It was too late to deny her presence; and as he entered, she said with a sort of excited confusion: "You did not keep your word!" "I promised nothing," he answered. "But you should have complied at least for my sake," she continued. "I asked you for the sake of your peace of mind and my own."

She scarcely knew what she said or did, and sent for some friends in order not to be alone with Werther. He put down several books he had brought with him, then enquired about some others, until she began to hope that her friends might arrive shortly and at the same time that they might stay away. The maid came back to say that neither friend could come.

For a moment she felt that the girl, with whatever work she had to do, should remain in the adjoining room, but she changed her mind. Werther, meanwhile, walked impatiently up and down. She went to the piano, and began to play a minuet—but it did not sound right. She pulled herself together and sat down quietly beside Werther, who had taken his usual place on the sofa.

"Have you brought nothing to read?" she enquired. He had nothing. "There in my drawer," she continued, "is your own translation of some of the songs of Ossian. I have not read them yet, I always hoped to hear you recite them; but it never seemed possible to arrange it." He smiled, and fetched the manuscript. A tremor ran through him as he took it in his hand, and his eyes were filled with tears as he looked at it. He sat down and read.

"Star of descending night! fair is thy light in the west! thou liftest thy unshorn head from thy cloud; thy steps are stately on thy hill. What dost thou behold in the plain? The stormy winds are laid. The murmur of the torrent comes from afar. Roaring waves climb the distant rock. The flies of evening are on their feeble wings; the hum of their course is on the field. What dost thou behold, fair light? But thou dost smile and depart. Thy waves come with joy around thee; they bathe thy lovely hair. Farewell, thou silent beam! Let the light of Ossian's soul arise!

"And it does arise in its strength! I behold my departed friends. Their gathering is on Lora, as in the days of other years. Fingal comes like a watery column of mist! his heroes are around; and see the bards of song—gray-haired Ullin! stately Ryno. Alpin with the tuneful voice! the soft complaint of Minona! How are ye changed, my friends, since the days of Selma's feast, when we contended, like gales of spring as they fly along the hill, and bend by turns the feebly whistling grass!

"Minona came forth in her beauty, with downcast look and tearful eye. Her hair flew slowly on the blast that rushed unfrequent from the hill. The souls of the heroes were sad when she raised the tuneful voice. Often had they seen the grave of Salgar, the dark dwelling of white-bosomed Colma. Colma left alone on the hill, with all her voice of song! Salgar promised to come; but the night descended around. Hear the voice of Colma, when she sat alone on the hill!

"*Colma:* It is night; I am alone, forlorn on the hill of storms. The wind is heard on the mountain. The torrent is howling down the rock. No hut receives me from the rain; forlorn on the hill of winds!

"Rise, moon, from behind thy clouds! Stars of the night, arise! Lead me, some light, to the place where my love rests from the chase alone! His bow near him unstrung, his dogs panting around him! But here I must sit alone by the rock of the mossy stream. The stream and the wind roar aloud. I hear not the voice of my love! Why delays my Salgar; why the chief of the hill his promise? Here is the rock, and here the tree; here is the roaring stream! Thou didst promise with night to be here. Ah, whither is my Salgar gone? With thee I would fly from my father, with thee from my brother of pride. Our race have long been foes: we are not foes, O Salgar!

"Cease a little while, O wind! stream, be thou silent awhile! Let my voice be heard around; let my wanderer hear me! Salgar! it is Colma who calls. Here is the tree and the rock. Salgar, my love, I am here! Why delayest thou thy coming? Lo! the calm moon comes forth. The flood is bright in the vale; the rocks are gray on the steep. I see him not on the brow. His dogs come not before him with tidings of his near approach. Here I must sit alone?

"Who lie on the heath beside me? Are they my love and my brother? Speak to me, O my friends! To Colma they give no reply. Speak to me: I am alone! My soul is tormented with fears. Ah, they are dead! Their swords are red from the fight. Oh, my brother! my brother! why hast thou slain my Salgar? Why, O Salgar! hast thou slain my brother? Dear were ye both to me! what shall I say in your praise? Thou wert fair on the hill among thousands! he was terrible in fight! Speak to me! hear my voice! hear me, sons of my love! They are silent, silent forever! Cold, cold, are their breasts of clay! Oh, from the rock on the hill, from the top of the windy steep, speak, ye ghosts of the dead! Speak, I will not be afraid! Whither are ye gone to rest? In what cave of the hill shall I find the departed? No feeble voice is on the gale: no answer half drowned in the storm!

"I sit in my grief: I wait for morning in my tears! Rear the tomb, ye friends of the dead. Close it not till Colma comes. My life flies away like a dream. Why should I stay behind? Here shall I rest with my friends, by the stream of the sounding rock. When night comes on the hill—when the loud winds arise, my ghost shall stand in the blast, and mourn the death of my friends. The hunter shall hear from his booth; he shall fear, but love my voice! For sweet shall my voice be for my friends: pleasant were her friends to Colma.

"Such was thy song, Minona, softly blushing daughter of

Torman. Our tears descended for Colma, and our souls were sad! Ullin came with his harp; he gave the song of Alpin. The voice of Alpin was pleasant; the soul of Ryno was a beam of fire! But they had rested in the narrow house; their voice had ceased in Selma! Ullin had returned one day from the chase before the heroes fell. He heard their strife on the hill; their song was soft, but sad! They mourned the fall of Morar, first of mortal men! His soul was like the soul of Fingal; his sword like the sword of Oscar. But he fell, and his father mourned; his sister's eyes were full of tears. Minona's eyes were full of tears, the sister of car-borne Morar. She retired from the song of Ullin, like the moon in the west, when she foresees the shower, and hides her fair head in a cloud. I touched the harp with Ullin; the song of mourning rose!

"*Ryno:* The wind and the rain are past; calm is the noon of day. The clouds are divided in heaven. Over the green hills flies the inconstant sun. Red through the stony vale comes down the stream of the hill. Sweet are thy murmurs, O stream! but more sweet is the voice I hear. It is the voice of Alpin, the son of song, mourning for the dead! Bent is his head of age; red his tearful eye. Alpin, thou son of song, why alone on the silent hill? why complainest thou, as a blast in the wood, as a wave on the lonely shore?

"*Alpin:* My tears, O Ryno! are for the dead—my voice for those that have passed away. Tall thou art on the hill; fair among the sons of the vale. But thou shalt fall like Morar; the mourner shall sit on thy tomb. The hills shall know thee no more; thy bow shall lie in thy hall unstrung!

"Thou wert swift, O Morar! as a roe on the desert; terrible as a meteor of fire. Thy wrath was as the storm; thy sword in battle as lightning in the field. Thy voice was a stream after rain, like thunder on distant hills. Many fell by thy arm: they were consumed in the flames of thy wrath. But when thou didst return from war, how peaceful was thy brow! Thy face was like the sun after rain, like the moon in the silence of night; calm as the breast of the lake when the loud wind is laid.

"Narrow is thy dwelling now! dark the place of thine abode! With three steps I compass thy grave, O thou who wast so great before! Four stones, with their heads of moss, are the only memorial of thee. A tree with scarce a leaf, long grass which whistles in the wind, mark to the hunter's eye the grave of the mighty Morar. Morar! thou are low indeed. Thou hast no mother to mourn thee, no maid with her tears of love. Dead is she that brought thee forth. Fallen is the daughter of Morglan.

"Who on his staff is this? Who is this whose head is white with age, whose eyes are red with tears, who quakes at every step? It is thy father, O Morar! the father of no son but thee. He heard of thy fame in war, he heard of foes dispersed. He heard of Morar's renown; why did he not hear of his wound? Weep, thou father of Morar! Weep, but thy son heareth thee not. Deep is the sleep of the dead—low their pillow of dust. No more shall he hear thy voice—no more awake at thy call. When shall it be morn in the grave, to bid the slumberer awake? Farewell, thou bravest of men! thou conqueror in the field! but the field shall see thee no more, nor the dark wood be lightened with the splendor of thy steel. Thou hast left no son. The song shall preserve thy name. Future times shall hear of thee—they shall hear of the fallen Morar!

"The grief of all arose, but most the bursting sigh of Armin. He remembers the death of his son, who fell in the days of his youth. Carmor was near the hero, the chief of the echoing Galmal. Why burst the sigh of Armin? he said. Is there a cause to mourn? The song comes with its music to melt and please the soul. It is like soft mist that, rising from a lake, pours on the silent vale; the green flowers are filled with dew, but the sun returns in his strength, and the mist is gone. Why art thou sad, O Armin, chief of sea-surrounded Gorma?

"Sad I am, nor small is my cause of woe! Carmor, thou hast lost no son; thou hast lost no daughter of beauty. Colgar the valiant lives, and Annira, fairest maid. The boughs of thy house ascend, O Carmor! But Armin is the last of his race. Dark is thy bed, O Daura! deep thy sleep in the tomb! When shalt thou wake with thy songs—with all thy voice of music?

"Arise, winds of autumn, arise; blow along the heath! Streams of the mountains, roar; roar, tempests in the groves of my oaks! Walk through broken clouds, O moon! show thy pale face at intervals; bring to my mind the night when all my children fell—when Arindal the mighty fell, when Daura the lovely failed. Daura, my daughter, thou wert fair—fair as the moon on Fura, white as the driven snow, sweet as the breathing gale. Arindal, thy bow was strong, thy spear was swift on the field, thy look was like mist on the wave, thy shield a red cloud in a storm! Armar, renowned in war, came and sought Daura's love. He was not long refused: fair was the hope of their friends.

"Erath, son of Odgal, repined: his brother had been slain by Armar. He came disguised like a son of the sea; fair was his skiff on the wave, white his locks of age, calm his serious brow. Fairest of women, he said, lovely daughter of Armin! a rock not distant in the sea bears a tree on its side: red shines the fruit afar. There Armar waits for Daura. I come to carry his love! She went—she called on Armar. Naught answered, but the son of the rock. Armar, my love, my love! why tormentest thou me with fear? Hear, son of Arnart, hear! it is Daura who calleth thee. Erath, the traitor, fled laughing to the land. She lifted up her voice—she called for her brother and her father. Arindal! Armin! none to relieve you, Daura.

"Her voice came over the sea. Arindal, my son, descended from the hill, rough in the spoils of the chase. His arrows rattled by his side; his bow was in his hand, five dark-gray dogs attended his steps. He saw fierce Erath on the shore; he seized and bound him to an oak. Thick wind the thongs of the hide around his limbs; he loads the winds with his groans. Arindal ascends the deep in his boat to bring Daura to land. Armar

116

came in his wrath, and let fly the gray-feathered shaft. It sung, it sunk in thy heart, O Arindal, my son! for Erath the traitor thou diest. The oar is stopped at once: he panted on the rock and expired. What is thy grief, O Daura, when round thy feet is poured thy brother's blood? The boat is broken in twain. Armar plunges into the sea to rescue his Daura, or die. Sudden a blast from a hill came over the waves; he sank, and he rose no more.

"Alone, on the sea-beat rock, my daughter was heard to complain; frequent and loud were her cries. What could her father do? All night I stood on the shore: I saw her by the faint beam of the moon. All night I heard her cries. Loud was the wind; the rain beat hard on the hill. Before morning appeared, her voice was weak; it died away like the evening breeze among the grass of the rocks. Spent with grief, she expired, and left thee, Armin, alone. Gone is my strength in war, fallen my pride among women. When the storms aloft arise, when the north lifts the wave on high, I sit by the sounding shore, and look on the fatal rock.

"Often by the setting moon I see the ghosts of my children; half viewless they walk in mournful conference together."

———◆———

A torrent of tears which streamed from Charlotte's eyes, and gave relief to her oppressed heart, stopped Werther's reading. He threw down the sheets, seized her hand, and wept bitterly. Charlotte leaned upon her other arm, and buried her face in her handkerchief; both were terribly agitated. They felt their own fate in the misfortunes of Ossian's heroes—felt this together, and merged their tears. Werther's eyes and lips burned on Charlotte's arm; she trembled, she wished to go, but grief and pity lay like a leaden weight upon her. She took a deep breath, recovered herself, and begged Werther, sobbing, to continue— implored him with the very voice of Heaven! He trembled, his heart ready to burst; then taking up the sheets again, he read in a broken voice: "Why dost thou awake me, O breath of Spring, thou dost woo me and say, 'I cover thee with the drops of heaven'? But the time of my fading is near, the blast that shall scatter my leaves. Tomorrow shall the traveller come; he that saw me in my beauty shall come. His eyes will search the field, but they will not find me."

The whole force of these words fell upon the unfortunate Werther. In deepest despair, he threw himself at Charlotte's feet, seized her hands, and pressed them to his eyes and to his forehead. An apprehension of his terrible plan seemed to strike her. Her thoughts were confused: she held his hands, pressed them to her bosom; and, turning toward him with the tenderest expression, her burning cheek touched his. They lost sight of everything. The world vanished before them. He clasped her in his arms tightly, and covered her trembling, stammering lips with furious kisses. "Werther!" she cried with choking voice, turning away. "Werther!" and, with a feeble hand, pushed him from her. And again, more composed and from the depth of her heart, she repeated, "Werther!" He did not resist, released her, and threw himself before her. Charlotte rose, and with confusion and grief, trembling between love and resentment, she exclaimed, "This is the last time, Werther! You shall never see me again!" Then, casting one last, loving glance at the unhappy man, she rushed into the adjoining room and locked the door. Werther held out his arms, but did not dare to detain her. He lay on the floor, with his head resting on the sofa, for half an hour, till he heard a noise which brought him to his senses. It was the maid, who wanted to lay the table. He walked up and down the room; and when he was alone, he went to Charlotte's door, and, in a low voice, said, "Charlotte, Charlotte! but one word more, one last adieu!" She did not answer. He waited, pleaded again, and waited. Finally he tore himself away, crying, "Adieu, Charlotte, adieu forever!"

He came to the town gate. The guards, who knew him, let him out without a word. It was raining and snowing. He knocked at the gate again at about eleven. His servant saw him enter the house without his hat but did not dare to say anything. As he undressed his master, he found that his clothes were wet. His hat was afterward found on the point of a rock overhanging the valley; and it is inconceivable how he could have climbed to the summit on such a dark, stormy night without losing his life.

He went to bed and slept late. The next morning his servant, who brought in his coffee, found him writing. He added the following passage to his letter to Charlotte.

———◆———

"For the last, last time, I open these eyes. Alas! they will see the sun no more. A dim and misty day hides it. Yes, Nature! Mourn; your friend, your lover, draws near his end! There is nothing like this feeling, Charlotte, and yet, it is most akin to a diffused dream, when you say to yourself—This is the last morning! The last! Charlotte, no word can adequately express this feeling. The last! Here I stand in all my strength—tomorrow I shall lie outstretched and inert. To die! What does it mean? We are but dreaming when we speak of death. I have seen many people die; but, so limited is our nature that we have no clear conception of the beginning or the end of our life. At this moment I am my own—or rather I belong to you, my beloved!— and the next we are parted, severed—perhaps forever! No, Charlotte, no! How can I, how can you, pass away so completely? We *are!* Pass away . . . a mere word, an empty sound, without feeling. Dead, Charlotte! laid in the cold earth, in the dark and narrow grave! There was a girl who was everything to me in my helpless youth. She died. I followed her hearse and stood by her grave when the coffin was lowered; when I heard the creaking of the ropes as they were loosened and drawn up, when the first shovelful of earth was thrown in, and the melancholy coffin returned a muffled sound, which grew fainter and fainter till all was completely covered over, I threw myself beside the grave; my heart was shaking, moved, shattered; my soul torn—but I knew not what had happened, what was to happen to me. Death! the grave! I do not understand the words. Forgive, oh, forgive me! Yesterday! it should have been the last day of my life! You angel!—for the first—first time in my life I felt rapture glow within my inmost soul. She loves, she loves me! The sacred fire of your lips still burns upon mine. New torrents of delight overwhelm my soul. Forgive me, forgive!

"I knew that you loved me; I knew from the first entrancing look, the first pressure of your hand; but when I was away from you, when I saw Albert at your side, my doubts and fears returned.

"Do you remember the flowers you sent me, when at that dreadful party you could neither speak to me nor give me your hand? Half the night I was on my knees before those flowers; they were to me the pledges of your love; but those impressions faded, as the believer gradually loses the sense of grace which his God conveyed to him so abundantly in sacred, visible symbols.

"All this passes away; but no eternity could extinguish the living flame which was kindled yesterday by your lips, and which now burns within me. She loves me! These arms have embraced her, these lips have trembled upon hers. She is mine! Yes, Charlotte, you are mine forever!

"And what does it mean that Albert is your husband? He may be, in this world; and in this world is it a sin to love you, to wish to tear you from his embrace? A sin? Very well! I suffer the punishment, but I have tasted the full delight of my sin. I have drunk a balm that has restored my soul. From this moment on you are mine; yes, Charlotte, mine! I go before you. I go to my Father, to your Father. I will bring my sorrows before Him, and He will give me comfort till you come. Then will I fly to meet you. I will hold you, and remain with you in eternal embrace, in the sight of the Infinite.

"I do not dream. So near the grave, I see more clearly. We *shall* exist; we shall see each other again; see your mother; I shall find her, and pour out my inmost heart to her. Your mother—your image!"

———————◆———————

About eleven o'clock Werther asked his servant if Albert had returned. He answered: "Yes," he had seen his horse go past; upon which Werther sent him the following note, unsealed:

"Would you lend me your pistols for a journey I am about to undertake? Adieu."

Charlotte had slept little that night. Her fears were realized in a way that she could neither have foreseen nor have avoided. She, who was usually so tranquil, was feverishly disturbed. A thousand painful sensations rent her heart. Was it the passion of Werther's embraces? Was it anger at his daring? Was it the contrast between her present condition with those days of innocence, peace and self-confidence? How could she face her husband, and confess a scene which she had no reason to conceal, and which she yet felt unwilling to avow? They had so long preserved a silence toward each other—and should she be the first to break it by this unexpected admission? She was afraid that the very news of Werther's visit would annoy him, and now—this sudden catastrophe! Dared she hope that he would see her in the true light and judge her without prejudice? Should she wish that he read her inmost soul? On the other hand, could she deceive him to whom all her thoughts had ever been as clear as a crystal, and from whom she never would or could conceal a single thought? All this made her anxious and distressed. Again and again her mind returned to Werther, who was now lost to her, but whom she could not bring herself to let go, and for whom she knew nothing was left but despair if she should be lost to him.

A shadow of that estrangement which had lately come between herself and Albert fell over her thoughts. Two such intelligent and well-meaning people had begun to keep silent because of certain unspoken differences of opinion—each preoccupied with his own right and the other's wrong, making things worse and worse until eventually it became impossible to disentangle the knot at the crucial moment on which all seemed to depend. If mutual trust had earlier brought them together again, if love and understanding had helped them open their hearts to each other, our friend might still have been saved.

But we must not forget one other curious circumstance. As we can gather from Werther's correspondence, he had never concealed his anxious desire to quit this world. He had often discussed the subject with Albert; and between Charlotte and Werther it had often been a topic of conversation. Albert was so opposed to the very idea that, with a kind of irritation unusual in him, he had more than once given Werther to understand that he doubted the seriousness of his threats, and not only turned them into ridicule but persuaded Charlotte to share his feelings. Her heart was thus fairly at ease when she thought of the melancholy subject, but she never communicated to her husband the fears she felt at that time.

Albert returned and was greeted by Charlotte with an embarrassed embrace. He was himself in a bad mood; his business was unfinished, and he had found the neighboring official, with whom he had to deal, an obstinate and narrow-minded person. The bad roads, too, had provoked him.

He enquired whether anything had happened during his absence, and Charlotte hastily answered that Werther had been there on the evening before. He then asked for his letters, and was answered that several packages had been left in his study. He thereupon retired, leaving Charlotte alone.

The presence of her husband, whom she loved and honored, made a fresh impression on her heart. The recollection of his generosity, kindness, and affection calmed her agitation; a secret impulse prompted her to follow him; she took her work and went to his study, as was often her custom. He was busy opening and reading his letters. It seemed as if some of them contained disagreeable news. She asked some question; he gave short answers and went to his desk to write.

Several hours passed, and Charlotte's feelings became more and more melancholy. She felt the extreme difficulty of explaining to her husband, even if he were in a better mood, the weight that lay upon her heart; and her depression became all the more distressing as she tried to hide her grief and to control her tears.

The arrival of Werther's boy caused her the greatest embarrassment. He gave Albert a note, which the latter coldly handed to his wife, saying, "Give him the pistols—I wish him a pleasant journey," he added, turning to the servant. These words fell upon Charlotte like thunder; she rose from her seat, half conscious of what she did. She walked slowly to the wall, took down the pistols with a trembling hand, wiped the dust from them, and hesitated. She would have delayed longer had not Albert hastened her by an impatient look. She gave the fatal weapons to the boy without being able to utter a word. As soon as he had gone, she folded up her work and went to her room, in a state of immeasurable uncertainty. Her heart prophesied all sorts of catastrophes. At one moment she was on the point of going to her husband, throwing herself at his feet, and confessing everything: all that had happened on the previous evening, her own guilt, her apprehensions; then she saw that such a step would be useless; she could not hope to induce Albert to visit Werther. The table was laid; and a kind friend who had come to ask a question or two helped to sustain the conversation. They pulled themselves together, talked about this and that, and were able to forget.

When the servant brought the pistols to Werther, the latter received them with transports of delight when he heard that Charlotte had given them to him with her own hand. He had bread and wine brought in, sent his servant to dinner, and then sat down to write:

"They have passed through your hands—you have wiped the dust from them. I kiss them a thousand times—you have touched them. Heavenly Spirits favor my design—and you, Charlotte, offer me the weapon. You, from whose hands I wished to receive my death. Now—my wish is gratified. I asked my servant. You trembled when you gave him the pistols, but you bade me no farewell. Alas, alas! Not one farewell! How could you shut your heart against me on account of that one moment which made you mine forever? Oh, Charlotte, ages cannot efface the impression—I feel you cannot hate him who loves you so!"

After dinner he called his servant, told him to finish packing, destroyed many papers, and then went out to settle some small debts. He returned home, then went out again beyond the gate in spite of the rain, walked for some time in the Count's garden, and farther into the neighborhood. Toward evening he came back and wrote:

"Wilhelm, I have for the last time seen fields, wood, and sky. Farewell, you, too! And you, dearest mother, forgive me! Console her, Wilhelm. God bless you both! I have settled all my affairs! Farewell! We shall meet again, and be happier."

"I have ill rewarded you, Albert; but you will forgive me. I have disturbed the peace of your house. I have sowed distrust between you. Farewell! I will end it all. And oh! that my death may restore your happiness! Albert, Albert! make the angel happy, and may God's blessing be upon you!"

He spent the rest of the evening going through his papers;

he tore and burned a great many; he sealed a few packages and addressed them to Wilhelm. They contained some short essays and disconnected aphorisms, some of which I have seen. At ten o'clock he ordered his fire to be made up, and a bottle of wine to be brought to him. He then sent his servant to bed; his room, as well as the apartments of the rest of the domestics, was situated in the back of the house. The boy lay down without undressing that he might be the sooner ready for his journey in the morning, as his master had told him that the coach horses would be at the door before six o'clock.

"After eleven

"All is silent around me, and my soul is calm. I thank Thee, God, that Thou hast given me strength and courage in these last moments! I step to the window, my dearest, and can see a few stars through the passing storm clouds. No, you will not fall. The Almighty sustains you, and me. I see the brightest lights of the Great Bear, my favorite constellation. When I left you, Charlotte, and went out from your gate, it always was in front of me. With what rapture have I so often looked at it! How many times have I implored it with raised hands to witness my happiness! and still—But what is there, Charlotte, that does not remind me of you? Are you not everywhere about me? and have I not, like a child, treasured up every trifle which your saintly hands have touched?

"Beloved silhouette! I now return it to you; and I pray you to preserve it. Thousands of kisses have I pressed upon it, and a thousand times did it gladden my heart when I have left the house or returned.

"I have asked your father in a note to protect my body. At one corner of the churchyard, looking towards the fields, there are two linden trees—there I wish to lie. Your father can, and doubtless will, do this for his friend. You ask him, too! I will not expect it of pious Christians that their bodies should be buried near the corpse of a poor, unhappy wretch like me. I could wish to lie in some remote valley by the wayside, where priest and Levite may bless themselves as they pass by my tomb, and the Samaritan shed a tear.

"See, Charlotte, I do not shudder to take the cold and fatal cup, from which I shall drink the draught of death. Your hand gave it to me, and I do not tremble. All, all the wishes and the hopes of my life are fulfilled. Cold and stiff I knock at the brazen gates of Death.

"Oh that I might have enjoyed the bliss of dying for you! how gladly would I have sacrificed myself for you, Charlotte! And could I but restore your peace and happiness, with what resolution, with what joy, would I not meet my fate! But it is given to but a chosen few to shed their blood for those they loved, and by their death to kindle a hundred-fold the happiness of those by whom they are beloved.

"Charlotte, I wish to be buried in the clothes I wear at present; you have touched them, blessed them. I have begged this same favor of your father. My spirit soars above my coffin. I do not wish my pockets to be searched. This pink bow which you wore the first time I saw you, surrounded by the children— Oh, kiss them a thousand times for me, and tell them the fate of their unhappy friend! I think I see them playing around me. The darling children! How they swarm about me! How I attached myself to you, Charlotte! From the first hour I saw you, I knew I could not leave you! Let this ribbon be buried with me; it was a present from you on my birthday. How eagerly I accepted it all! I did not think that it would all lead to this! Be calm! I beg you, be calm!

"They are loaded—the clock strikes twelve. So be it! Charlotte! Charlotte, farewell, farewell!"

A neighbor saw the flash, and heard the shot; but, as everything remained quiet, he thought no more of it.

At six in the morning, the servant entered Werther's room with a candle. He found his master stretched on the floor, blood about him, and the pistol at his side. He called to him, took him in his arms, but there was no answer, only a rattling in the throat. The servant ran for a surgeon, for Albert. Charlotte heard the bell; a shudder seized her. She awakened her husband; both arose. The servant, in tears, stammered the dreadful news. Charlotte fell senseless at Albert's feet.

When the surgeon arrived, Werther was lying on the floor; his pulse beat, but his limbs were paralyzed. The bullet had entered the forehead over the right eye; his brains were protruding. He was bled in the arm; the blood came, and he breathed.

From the blood on the chair, it could be inferred that he had committed the deed sitting at his desk, and that he had afterwards fallen on the floor and had twisted convulsively around the chair. He was found lying on his back near the window. He was fully dressed in his boots, blue coat and yellow waistcoat.

The house, the neighbors, and the whole town were in commotion. Albert arrived. They had laid Werther on the bed. His head was bandaged, and the pallor of death was upon his face. His limbs were motionless; a terrible rattling noise came from his lungs, now strongly, now weaker. His death was expected at any moment.

He had drunk only one glass of the wine. "Emilia Galotti" lay open on his desk.

Let me say nothing of Albert's distress or of Charlotte's grief.

The old judge hastened to the house upon hearing the news; he kissed his dying friend amid a flood of tears. His eldest boys soon followed him on foot. In speechless sorrow they threw themselves on their knees by the bedside, and kissed his hands and face. The eldest, who was his favorite, clung to his lips till he was gone; even then the boy had to be taken away by force. At noon Werther died. The presence of the judge, and the arrangements he had made prevented a disturbance; that night, at the hour of eleven he had the body buried in the place that Werther had chosen.

The old man and his sons followed the body to the grave. Albert could not. Charlotte's life was in danger. The body was carried by workmen. No clergyman attended.

The New Melusina

The New Melusina[1]

HONORED GENTLEMEN: since I know you care very
little for introductory remarks or preambles, I shall at once
assure you that this time I hope to conduct myself in a highly
proper manner. I admit that in the past I have given out many
true stories which have proven satisfactory to everyone; but
today I boldly assert that I have one to relate which far sur-
passes all previous tales; one which, although it happened to
me several years ago, still makes me uneasy whenever I remember it, awakening the hope for some final resolution. It
would be difficult for you to match it.

Before all, it must be confessed that I have not always so
planned my life as to insure my immediate future, or even my
next day. In my youth I was not a good manager, and often
found myself in various straits. Once I set out upon a journey
which should have proved highly profitable; but I cut my cloth
too big, and after starting out in a private post-chaise had to
continue in the public stage-coach, till at last I was obliged to
face the rest of the way on foot.

Being a quick-witted fellow, I had made a custom of seeking
out the landlady, or even the cook, as soon as I came to an inn,
and by treating them to a little flattery usually succeeded in
reducing my expenses. One evening as I was entering the post-
tavern of a small town, intent on pursuing my usual practise, a
handsome, two-seated carriage, drawn by four horses, rattled

[1] Translated by Jean Starr Untermeyer. Reprinted by permission of the trans-
lator and of Julian Messner, Inc., from *Strange to Tell: Stories of the Marvelous and
Mysterious,* edited by Marjorie Fischer and Rolfe Humphries; copyright, 1946, by
Julian Messner, Inc.

up to the door behind me. I turned around and saw a solitary young woman, unattended by a maid or servants. I made haste to open the door for her and to ask if I could be of service. As she stepped out she disclosed a beautiful figure and, on closer inspection, an amiable countenance marked by faint though not unpleasant traces of sadness. Again I inquired if I could in any way serve her. "Oh, yes," she said, "if you will lift out the little casket that lies on the seat and carry it in for me; but, I entreat you, hold it level and do not shift or shake it in the slightest degree." I took up the casket cautiously, she closed the carriage door, we ascended the steps together and she told the servants that she would remain overnight.

Now we were alone in the room; she directed me to place the casket on the table which stood near the wall, and inferring from certain of her movements that she wished to be alone, I took my leave, kissing her hand respectfully but ardently.

At that she said: "Order supper for us both," and I leave you to imagine with what satisfaction I carried out her bidding, so exalted that I scarcely deigned to glance at the landlady or the servants. Impatiently I waited for the moment that would bring me to her once more. Supper was served, we sat facing each other. For the first time in quite a while I regaled myself with a good meal and at the same time with a charming sight: indeed, it seemed to me that she became more beautiful with every minute.

Her conversation was engaging, yet she sought to reject everything pertaining to attraction or love. The table was cleared; I tarried, I tried every dodge to approach her—but in vain. She held me off with a certain dignity I could not withstand; indeed, against my will I was forced to leave her rather early.

After a night spent mostly in wakefulness, or filled with restless dreams. I arose early and asked whether the horses had been ordered. Upon being told "No," I walked into the garden where I saw her standing dressed at her window. I hastened to go up to her. As she came toward me, as beautiful, no, more beautiful than yesterday, I was suddenly overcome by desire, cunning and audacity; I rushed toward her and clasped her in my arms. "Heavenly, irresistible creature," I cried out, "forgive me, but it is impossible to withstand you!" With unbelievable agility she released herself before I had the chance even to press a kiss upon her cheek. "Restrain yourself from such abrupt and passionate outbreaks, unless you want to forgo a bit of good fortune that lies near you, but which can be obtained only after certain tests."

"Exact of me what you will, angelic spirit," I exclaimed, "but do not drive me to despair." She smiled as she answered: "If you wish to devote your services to me, hear the conditions. I came here to visit a woman friend and to spend a few days with her; meanwhile I would like my carriage and this little case to be brought further along the road. Would you care to undertake this? You will have nothing to do but to lift the case in and out of the carriage, to sit beside it and to be responsible for it. When you come to an inn you are to place it in a room by itself, in which you will neither sit nor sleep. You will lock the room each time with this key, which opens and closes every lock, and has the power of making it impossible for the lock to be opened by anyone in the meantime."

I looked at her, overcome by a feeling of strangeness; I promised her I would do everything if only I might hope to see her soon again, and if she would seal this hope by a kiss. She did so, and from that moment I became her bondsman. She told me that now I should order the horses. We discussed the road I should take as well as the place where I was to stop and await her. Finally she pressed a purse of gold into my hand, and I a kiss upon hers. At parting she seemed to be moved, and I was past knowing what I was doing or was about to do.

After I had given the order, I came back and found the door of the room locked. I tested my master-key and it performed perfectly. The door sprang open, the room was empty save for the casket which stood on the table where I had placed it.

The carriage had drawn to the door, I took down the casket solicitously and placed it beside me. The landlady asked, "But where is the lady?" and a child answered, "She went into the town." I took leave of the people and drove off, as it were in triumph, from the place where but last evening I had arrived with dust-covered leggings. You may take it for granted that now, completely at leisure, I reviewed the whole matter, counted the money, made all sorts of plans and occasionally glanced over at the casket. I kept straight on, passing several places, and did not halt until I reached the fair-sized town where she had directed me to meet her. Her commands were scrupulously obeyed; the casket was placed in a room by itself and a couple of wax candles lighted near it, just as she had ordered. I locked the room, got to rights in mine, and made myself fairly comfortable.

For a while I was engrossed in thoughts of her, but very soon time hung heavy on my hands. I was unaccustomed to living without companionship and presently I found some to my taste at the inn tables and in public places. Under these circumstances my money began to melt away, and one evening when I had recklessly yielded to a passionate fit of gambling it vanished completely from my purse. On coming back to my room I was beside myself. Without funds, while to all appearances a rich man, with the prospect of a heavy debt, uncertain as to whether or when my lovely one would show up, I was in the greatest dilemma. Now my longing for her was doubled, and I was convinced I could no longer live without her and her money.

After supper, for which I had little appetite, since now I was forced to eat alone, I paced quickly to and fro in my room, talking aloud to myself, upbraiding myself, throwing myself on the floor, tearing my hair and behaving in a most unruly fashion. Of a sudden I hear a soft movement in the locked room adjoining, and shortly after a knock on the well-guarded door.

I pull myself together, reach for the master key; but the folding-doors spring open of themselves, and in the gleam from the lighted tapers my lovely one approaches. I throw myself at her feet, kissing her dress, her hands; she raises me, but I lack courage to embrace her, almost to look at her; yet frankly though ruefully I confess my fault. "It is pardonable," she said, "only, alas, you delay your own good fortune as well as mine. Now you must again cover some ground in the world before we meet again. Here is more gold and it will suffice if you are disposed to be the least bit prudent. But if wine and women have proved your undoing this time, protect yourself hence-forth from both, and let me hope for a happy reunion."

She stepped back through the doorway, the folding-doors closed, I knocked, I entreated, but nothing more could be heard. Next morning when I asked for my account, the waiter smiled and said: "We know all right why you lock your doors in so artful and baffling a way that no master-key is able to open them. Our guess was that you had a lot of money and valuables; but now your treasure has been seen coming down the stairs, and from all accounts appeared worth being well-guarded."

To this I made no answer, but settling my account I entered the carriage with my casket. Once again I drove into the wide world, firmly resolved that in future I would heed the warning of my mysterious friend. Yet, almost as soon as I arrived at a large town, I made the acquaintance of some affable young women from whom I was utterly unable to tear myself away. They, it seemed, wished me to pay dearly for their favor, for although they constantly kept me at a distance, they led me from one expense to the other. And as I sought only to advance their pleasure, I never gave a second thought to my purse, but continued to pay out and to spend whenever the occasion arose. Consequently, I was astonished and overjoyed when, after a few weeks, I noticed that my purse showed no signs of shrink-age but was as bulky and bulging as at first. Since I wanted to make sure of this charming trait, I sat down to count up what I had, made a note of the precise amount, and began to live with my companions as gaily as before.

There were plenty of excursions by land and water, also dancing, and other pleasures, but now no great attention was called for to perceive that the purse was indeed dwindling, as if, through my deuced counting, I had filched from it the virtue of being uncountable. Meanwhile, the life of pleasure being in full swing, I could not back out, even though I was soon at the end of my cash. I cursed my state, calling out upon my friend for having led me into temptation, taking it ill of her that she failed to put in an appearance; angrily I declared myself free of all duties toward her and considered opening the casket on the chance that some help might be found in it. For, although it was not quite heavy enough to contain gold, yet it might hold jewels, and these too would be welcome. I was about to carry out my intention but decided to postpone it until the night, in order to undertake the operation in utter quiet, and ran off to a banquet which was just beginning. Things there were going full tilt and we were stirred up by the wine and the blaring of the trumpets when a stroke of ill-luck befell me: at dessert, a former friend of my favorite beauty returned unexpectedly from a journey, and sitting down beside her attempted with very little formality to claim his old privileges. This gave rise to ill-humor, disputes and brawling. We drew our swords, and I was carried home half dead from several wounds.

The surgeon had bandaged me and left; it was already late in the night and my attendant asleep when the door of the next room opened and my mysterious friend entered and seated herself beside my bed. She asked how I was; I did not answer, for I was worn and vexed. She went on speaking with much sympathy, rubbed my temples with a certain balsam, so that soon I felt decidedly stronger—so strong that I was able to arouse my anger and to chide her. Speaking impetuously, I threw all the blame for my misfortune upon her, on the passion she had awakened in me, on her appearance and her disappearance, on the tedium and on the longing that had been my portion. I became more and more violent, as though attacked by fever, and finally I swore to her that if she would not be mine, that if this time she refused to belong to me and be united with me, I had no further desire to live. And what is more, I demanded a decisive answer. As she hesitated, fencing with an explanation, I grew quite beside myself, and tore the double and triple bandages from my wounds with the fixed intention of bleeding to death. But how astonished I was when I found my wounds entirely healed, my body spruce and shining, and her in my arms!

We were now the happiest couple in the world. We asked each other's pardon without rightly knowing why. She promised now to travel with me, and soon we were sitting side by side in the carriage with the casket opposite in the place of a third person. I had never made any allusion to it, and even now it did not occur to me to speak of it to her, although there it stood, right before our eyes, and both of us, as occasion required, took charge of it as by an unspoken agreement, save that it was I who always lifted it in and out of the carriage and, as before, attended to locking the doors.

As long as something still remained in the purse I continued to do the paying; when my cash gave out I let her know it. "That is easy to provide," she said, and pointed to a pair of small pockets attached at both sides to the top of the carriage, which I had undoubtedly noticed before, but had never used. She reached into one and drew out a few gold pieces, and from the other several silver coins, thus showing me it was possible for us to continue spending as much as we liked. In this way we journeyed from town to town, from country to country, happy either to be by ourselves or with others, and it never occurred to me that she could leave me again, all the less so since for some time past she had certain hopes which would only add to our happiness and our love. But, alas, there came a morning when

I found she was not there, and since a sojourn without her was irksome to me, I took my casket and started to travel, tried out the powers of both pockets and found that they still held good.

The journey prospered, and if until now I had not reflected much on my adventure, since I expected these strange happenings to unravel themselves quite naturally, yet now something occurred which cast me into a state of astonishment, yes, even of fear. In order to get far away from a place it was my habit to travel day and night, and so it happened that often I drove in the dark, and if accidentally the lamps gave out, my carriage was in total blackness. Once on such a murky night I fell asleep, and on awakening saw the glimmer of a light on the ceiling of my carriage. I observed it and found that it came out of the casket which, because of the hot, dry weather of advancing summer, seemed to have sprung a rift. Again I started to speculate about the jewels; I fancied a carbuncle lying in the box and wished to make sure of it. Twisting myself around as well as I was able, I brought my eye in direct contact with the opening. But how great was my astonishment when I looked into a room brightly lit with candles and furnished with much taste, even magnificence, exactly as if I were looking down from an aperture in the ceiling into a drawing-room of royalty. It is true that I could see only a part of the room, but from that I could surmise the rest. An open fire seemed to be burning on the hearth and near it stood an arm-chair. I held my breath and continued looking. Meanwhile a young woman with a book in her hand approached from the other side of the room, and immediately I recognized her as my wife, although her figure had shrunk to the smallest proportions. The beautiful creature seated herself in the chair near the fireplace to read, and as she arranged the logs with the neatest pair of tongs I could plainly see that this most adorable of little beings was about to become a mother. Now, however, I found it necessary to move slightly from my uncomfortable position, and immediately after, just as I was on the point of looking in again to convince myself that it had not been a dream, the light went out and I peered into blank darkness.

My amazement and terror can easily be imagined. I formed a thousand theories about this discovery, and yet I could think out nothing. In this turmoil I fell asleep and when I awoke I believed I had only dreamed it all. Yet I felt somewhat estranged from my lovely one, and although I carried the casket with ever greater care, I knew not whether her reappearance in full human dimensions was more to be dreaded than desired.

After a while, toward evening, my lovely one actually came to me, dressed in white, and as the room was just getting dark she seemed taller to me than she usually appeared, and I remembered having heard that all from the race of pixies and gnomes noticeably increase in stature with the coming of night. She rushed into my arms as she always did, but I was unable to clasp her to my uneasy breast with complete joy.

"My dearest," she said, "the way you receive me confirms me in feeling what I, alas, already know. You have seen me in the interval; you have learned of the state in which at certain times I find myself. This causes a break in your happiness and also in mine, which indeed is on the point of being utterly destroyed. I must leave you, and I do not know if I shall ever see you again." Her presence, the charm with which she spoke, at once removed nearly all recollection of that sight which even before had appeared in my mind's eye like a dream. Impulsively I embraced her, convinced her of my passion, assured her of my innocence and told her the accidental nature of my discovery; in short, I did everything that seemed to quiet her and she in turn tried to bring me calm.

"Test yourself thoroughly," she said, "to see whether this discovery has not blighted your love, whether you can forget that I live with you in two forms, and whether the diminution in my person will not diminish your affection as well."

I looked at her; she was more beautiful than ever, and I

thought to myself: "Is it then such a great misfortune to possess a wife who from time to time becomes a pygmy, so that one can carry her around in a box? Would it not be far worse were she to become a giantess and clap her husband into the box?" My serenity returned. Not for anything in the world would I have let her go. "Dear heart," I answered, "let us remain and continue to be as we have been. Could we find anything more delightful? Consult your own comfort and I promise to carry the casket all the more carefully. How could I retain a bad impression from the prettiest spectacle I have ever seen in my whole life? How happy all lovers, could they possess such miniature pictures! And after all it was merely such a picture, a little conjuring trick. You are just sounding me, teasing me; however you shall see how I shall acquit myself."

"The matter is graver than you think," said the lovely creature; "meanwhile I am quite content that you take it so lightly; for it may still turn out quite happily for us both. I shall trust to you, and for my part I shall do whatever is possible; only promise me never to think back on this discovery with reproach. In addition, I earnestly beg you to beware more than ever of anger and of wine."

I promised what she desired; I would have gone on promising anything and everything; but she herself changed the subject, and everything ran smoothly as before. There was no reason for us to move from the place where we were staying; the town was large, the society varied, the season favorable for country jaunts and garden parties.

At all such festivities my wife was greatly in demand, much sought after by both men and women. A kind and ingratiating manner together with a certain nobility made her loved and respected by everyone. Moreover, she played brilliantly on the lute, accompanying her own singing, and there was never a social evening but must be graced with her talent.

I may as well admit I have never derived a great deal from music; on the contrary, its effect upon me was often unpleasant.

Therefore my lovely one, who had observed my reactions in this respect, never tried so to entertain me when we were alone; however, she seemed to find compensation for this when in company where she usually found a host of adorers.

And now—why should I deny it?—our last conversation had not sufficed entirely to dispel the matter, notwithstanding my best intentions; rather had it induced in me an unwonted sensitivity of feeling of which I was not wholly aware. So one evening at a large gathering my restrained ill-humor burst forth, which redounded to my great disadvantage.

Looking back upon the matter dispassionately, I acknowledge that I loved my charmer far less after that unhappy discovery, and now I was becoming jealous of her, a feeling which was new to me. This particular evening as we sat at table, diagonally across though fairly far from one another, I found myself quite content with both my supper-partners, a couple of young women whom for some time past I had found most attractive. What with jesting and sentimental sallies, we were not sparing of the wine; meanwhile at the other side of the table, a pair of music lovers had managed to persuade my wife, and to encourage and lead on the guests to participate in singing, both solo and in chorus. The two amateurs seemed importunate; the singing made me irritable, and when they demanded that even I should sing a solo stanza, I became really enraged, drained my glass and banged it on the table.

Although the charms of my neighbors soon calmed me again, still it is a bad thing for anger to get out of control. I boiled inwardly, although everything was conducive to pleasure and relaxation. On the contrary, I grew still more petulant when, a lute having been brought, my lovely one accompanied her song to everyone else's admiration. Unfortunately, a general silence was requested. This put an end to my chatter, while the sounds set my teeth on edge. Was it any wonder, then, that the smallest spark set off the mine?

The singers had barely finished a song amid the greatest

applause when she looked over to me most lovingly. Unhappily, her glance did not reach my heart. She observed that I gulped down my glass of wine and filled it up again. She warned me affectionately by wagging the forefinger of her right hand. "Remember it is wine!" she said, just loud enough for me to hear. "Water is for nixies!" I exclaimed. "Ladies," she called to my supper-partners, "encircle the goblet with every enchantment, so that it is not emptied so often." "Surely you will not let yourself be dictated to!" whispered one of them in my ear. "What's the imp after?" I called out, with an impetuous movement that overturned my glass. "A great deal is being wasted here!" cried the exquisite creature, plucking the strings of her lute as if to distract the attention of the company from this disturbance and draw it once more to herself. She actually succeeded in doing so, all the more as she stood up, but only as if to play with more comfort, and continued her prelude.

When I saw the red wine flowing over the table-cloth I came to my senses. I realized the great mistake I had made, and was inwardly repentent. For the first time music spoke to me. Her opening stanza was a friendly leave-taking from the company while they could still feel themselves together; with the one following the gathering seemed on the point of flowing apart; everyone felt himself alone, cut off; no one believed himself to be any longer present. But then, what should I say of the last stanza? It was addressed to me alone: the voice of offended love, bidding good-bye to ill-humor and presumption.

I led her home without a word, expecting nothing pleasant for myself. Yet, scarcely were we in our room when she proved herself most kind and charming, yes, even arch, making me the happiest of men.

The following morning, wholly solaced and full of love, I said: "Many a time you have sung, challenged to do so by good company, as for instance last night when you sang that touching song of farewell; now once, for my sake, sing a pretty and joyful song of welcome in this morning hour, so that it may seem as if we were learning to know each other for the first time."

"That, my friend, I may not do," she answered gravely. "Last night's song made allusion to our parting which must take place at once; for I can only tell you that the way you have violated your promise and your oath will result in calamity for us both: you lightly spurn a great gift of fortune, and even I must renounce my dearest wishes."

When, at this, I pressed her and pled with her to explain herself more clearly, she replied: "Unhappily, that is easy for me to do, since in any case the possibility of my remaining with you is over. Hear, then, what I would have preferred to conceal from you until our last moments together. The form in which you espied me in the little casket is really congenital and natural to me; for I am a lineal descendant of King Eckwald, the mighty prince of elves, of whom authentic history has so much to tell. As of old, our people are still active and industrious, and therefore easy to govern as well. But do not assume that the elves have remained backward in respect to their labors. Were this so their most famous products would still be swords which are able to pursue the enemy after whom they are thrown, chains which bind invisibly, mysteriously impenetrable shields, and things of this sort. Instead, their principal occupation now is making articles of convenience and adornment, in which they excel all other people on the earth. You would be amazed were you to pass through our workshops and warehouses. All of this would be highly satisfactory had not a strange circumstance arisen which affected the whole nation, but before all the royal family."

As she held back momentarily, I requested her to tell me more of these prodigious secrets, to which she complied.

"It is well known," she said, "that directly after God had created the world, when the soil was still dry and the mountains stood there mighty and majestic, that God, I say, proceeded before all things to create the elves, so that there might exist reasonable beings to gaze out from their clefts and burrows in wonder and reverence at His marvels within the earth. Furthermore, it is known that at a later time this little race undertook to exalt itself and to assume dominion over the earth. Wherefore God then created the dragons in order to drive the elves back into the mountains. But since the dragons themselves took care to settle down in the great caves and fissures and to live there, many of them spitting fire and working havoc in many other ways, the elves thus found themselves so hard-pressed and afflicted that they no longer knew where to come or go. Therefore they turned in humility and supplication to God, the Lord, calling out to Him and praying Him to exterminate this unclean breed of dragons. Yet, if in His wisdom He might not decide to destroy His own creatures, still the great plight of the poor elves so touched His heart that at once He created the giants who were to fight the dragons and if not to root them out, at least to reduce their number.

"But scarcely had the giants almost disposed of the dragons than their pride and presumption mounted, in consequence of which they too committed many atrocities, especially against the good little elves. They in their need turned again to the Lord. Then He in the might of His power created the knights who were to fight the giants and the dragons and live harmoniously with the elves. With this the work of creation was ended upon earth, and it came to pass thereafter that giants and dragons as well as knights and elves were able to coexist and bear with one another. From which you may infer, my friend, that ours is the oldest race in the world—an honor, no doubt, but one that brings us great disadvantages too.

"For since, as you know, nothing persists forever on this earth but, on the contrary, everything which has once been great must become small and less than it was, so it was in our case; since the beginning of the world we have continued to grow smaller and to fall away, and the royal family, because of the purity of its blood, was first and foremost to be subjected to this fate. Therefore, many years back, our wise men conceived of a plan to extricate us from our difficulty; from time to time a princess of the royal house was to be sent out into the world to take in marriage some honorable knight so that the race of pygmies might be rejuvenated and saved from complete decline."

As my lovely one spoke these words with complete candor, I looked at her uncertainly, because it seemed to me that she wished to play a little on my credulity. Concerning her dainty ancestry I had no further doubt; but it caused me some misgivings that she had seized on me instead of a knight, for I knew myself too well to be able to believe that my forebears had been directly created by God.

Concealing my amazement and doubt, I asked her kindly: "But tell me, my dear child, how do you come to have this tall and imposing form? For I know few women to compare with you in fineness of figure!" "That you shall learn," said my beauty. "From olden times we have been advised through the council of the elf-king to beware of taking this extraordinary step as long as possible, which to me seems natural and right. In all probability there would still have been much reluctance to sending a princess out into the world again, had not my younger brother been born so tiny that the nurses actually let him slip through his swaddling clothes and he was lost, and nobody knows what became of him. In this plight, hitherto quite unheard of in the annals of the elf-kingdom, our wise men were called together and, to make a long story short, they took a resolution to send me out to look for a husband."

"A resolution!" I cried. "That is all well and good. One may decide something for oneself, one may decree something for another, but to give a pygmy the stature of a goddess! How did your wise men accomplish that?"

"It was already provided for by our ancestors," she said. "In the royal treasury lay an enormous gold finger-ring.—I speak of it now as it appeared in the past when it was shown me, a child, in its natural surroundings; for it is the very same one that I have here on my finger.—At this point they went to work in the following manner: I was informed of everything that awaited me and was instructed what to do and what not to do.

"A magnificent palace, patterned after my parents' favorite summer residence, was constructed: a main building with side wings and everything one could wish for. It stood at the entrance to a large rocky ravine, adding greatly to its beauty. On the appointed day the court assembled there together with my parents and myself. The army was on parade, and twenty-four priests with no little difficulty bore the wonderful ring upon a precious barrow. It was placed upon the threshold of the building, just inside where one would step over it. Many ceremonies were performed and, after an affectionate leave-taking, I set to work. I stepped forward, laid my hand upon the ring, and at once began noticeably to increase in size. In a few moments I had attained my present height; whereupon I put the ring upon my finger. Now, in a trice, windows, doors and gates closed up, the wings at either side drew back into the main building, and near me, instead of a palace, stood a small casket which I at once picked up and took along with me, not without an agreeable sensation at being so large and strong. While yet a pygmy, to be sure, in comparison with trees and mountains, with streams and stretches of land, I was, however, a giant in comparison with grass and herbs, but especially with the ants who, since we pygmies were not always on good terms with them, took frequent occasion to plague us.

"How I fared on my pilgrimage before I met you, I might have much to tell. It will suffice to say that I put many to the test, but no one except yourself seemed to me worthy of refreshing and perpetuating the line of the sovereign Eckwald."

This recital gave some occasion for headshaking although I forbore to shake mine. I put various questions to which, however, I received no direct answers, but instead I learned to my great distress that after what had happened it was necessary for her to return to her parents. Certainly, she hoped to come back to me, but for the moment it was unavoidable that she present herself; otherwise all would be lost for her as well as for me. Soon the purses would cease paying, and all sorts of other consequences might follow.

Upon hearing that our money might give out, I made no further inquiries as to what else might happen. I shrugged my shoulders and said nothing, as she seemed to understand me.

Together we packed up and seated ourself in the carriage, and opposite to us was the casket in which I could still not discern anything resembling a palace. And so we went on, passing many places. Money for lodging and gratuities was easily and generously paid from the pockets to right and left, till at last we arrived at a mountainous region where scarcely had we alighted than my lovely one went on ahead and I, at her behest, followed with the casket. She guided me up a rather steep foot-path to a narrow strip of meadow through which a clear stream, now leaping, now loitering, wound its way. There she called my attention to a flat elevation, directed me to set down the case, and said: "Fare you well; you will easily find the way back; think of me, I hope to see you again."

At this moment it seemed to me impossible to leave her. She was just having one of her good days again, or, if you like, her good hours. To be alone with so lovable a creature on the green sward, amid grass and flowers, hemmed in by rocks, soothed by the sounds of water, what heart could have remained unmoved? I wished to take her hand, to clasp her in my arms, but she pushed me back, although most affectionately, threatening me with great peril if I did not leave at once.

"Is there not the remotest chance of my remaining?" I cried, "of your keeping me with you?" I accompanied these words with such gestures and sounds of lamentation that she seemed touched, and after some reflection admitted that it was not entirely impossible for our union to continue. Who was happier than I? My importunity, which became more and more pressing, obliged her to speak out and tell me that if I could decide to join her in being as small as I had already seen her, it was still not too late for me to remain with her, and pass over with her into her dwelling, her kingdom and her family. This prospect was not altogether pleasing to me; yet at this moment I could not quite tear myself away from her, and since for a considerable time I had been accustomed to the marvelous, and committed to hasty decisions, I assented, telling her she could do with me what she wished.

Thereupon I had to stretch out the little finger of my right hand, she placed her own against it, and drawing off the gold ring very gently with her left hand let it slip onto my finger. Scarcely had she done so when I felt a sharp pain in the finger; the ring contracted, torturing me horribly. I let out a scream and groped around me involuntarily for my lovely one, but she had vanished. My feelings in the meantime were inexpressible, and nothing more remains to be said than that very soon I found myself in a small, compact body near to my charmer in a forest of grass-blades. The joy of reunion after so short and yet so strange a parting or, if you prefer, a reunion without parting, passes all comprehension. I fell upon her neck, she returned my embraces, and the little couple felt as happy as the big one.

With some discomfort we set out to climb a hill; for the grassy meadow had become for us an almost impenetrable forest. But finally we reached a clearing, and how astonished I was to see there a large, symmetrical mass, which I was soon forced to recognize as the casket, in the same condition in which I had set it down.

"Go, my friend, and merely knock on it with the ring," said my sweetheart. "You will behold wonders." I walked up to it, and scarcely had I knocked before I witnessed the greatest marvel. Two side wings jutted out, and at the same time, like a shower of scales and shingles, various portions fell into place, revealing a complete palace, equipped with doors, windows and arcades.

A person who has seen one of Röntgen's ingenious writing-tables, so made that a slight tug brings into play a number of ratchets and springs, whereby desk, writing materials, drawers for letters and money come to view either simultaneously or one right after the other, will be able to picture to himself the unfolding of this palace into which my sweet companion now drew me. In the main hall I at once recognized the hearth which I had formerly glimpsed from above, and the chair on which she had sat. And when I looked overhead I thought I could still detect something of the rift in the dome through which I had looked in. I spare you a description of the rest; it is enough to say that all was spacious, costly and in good taste. Scarcely had I recovered from my amazement when I heard from afar the strains of martial music. My lovely half sprang up for joy and rapturously announced to me the approach of her royal father. We went and stood in the doorway and watched while a brilliant procession filed out of a high, rocky cleft. Soldiers, servants, household officials, and a shining array of courtiers followed one behind the other. At last we saw a gleaming galaxy and in its midst the king himself. When the whole procession had drawn up before the palace, the king advanced with his personal retainers. His affectionate daughter ran to meet him, dragging me along; we threw ourselves at his feet; he raised me most graciously, and it was only when I came to stand before him that I noticed that in this miniature world I was the most imposing in stature. Together we went toward the palace, where the king in the presence of his whole court addressed us in a well-prepared speech; expressing his astonishment at finding us here, he bade us welcome, acknowledged me as his son-in-law, and set the following day for the marriage-rites.

How terribly depressed I felt at the mention of marriage! for hitherto I had dreaded this almost more than music itself, which otherwise had seemed to me the most hateful thing on earth.

149

"Those people who make music," I was wont to say, "at least remain under the illusion of being at one with each other, and of working in unison: for when they have been tuning up long enough, rending our ears with all manner of discords, they are firm and fast in the conviction that their difficulties have been solved, and that one instrument is exactly in tune with the other. Even the director shares this happy delusion, and delightedly they start off, while the rest of us feel our ears buzzing from the constant din. In the wedded state, on the other hand, even this is not the case: for although it is only a duet, which would lead one to assume that two voices, or rather two instruments are bound to be brought into some degree of harmony, yet this seldom comes to pass. For if a man leads off with one tone, his wife at once takes a higher one; in this way they pass from chamber to choral pitch, on and on, getting higher and higher, until even the wind-instruments cannot follow. Therefore, since even harmonic music remains so offensive to me, it is still less conceivable that I should suffer the inharmonic."

Of the many festivities to which the day was given over, there is not much of which I would or can, speak: for I paid them scant attention. The sumptuous food, the delicious wines, nothing of this was to my taste. I speculated and pondered on what I should do. Yet I could think of little. I resolved that when the night came I would make short work of getting up and going off to hide somewhere. I succeeded in reaching a crevice in the rock into which I squirmed, concealing myself as well as I was able. My next care was to get the unlucky ring off my finger, in which I was not at all successful. On the contrary, I was made to feel that whenever I thought to take it off the ring became tighter, giving me acute twinges of pain, which subsided as soon as I desisted from my purpose.

I awoke in the early morning—for my little body had slept very well—and was on the point of looking around me a bit further when it seemed as if it had begun to rain. For something like sand or grit fell in large quantities through the grass, leaves and flowers; but how terrified I was when everything about me came alive, and an endless swarm of ants rushed down upon me. No sooner had they become aware of me than they attacked me from all sides, and though I defended myself well and courageously, yet finally they so overwhelmed, pinched and pricked me that I was glad when I heard myself called on to surrender. In truth, I did surrender at once, at which an ant of unusual size approached me with politeness, not to say reverence, and even commended himself to my favor. I found that the ants were allies of my father-in-law, and that he had called upon them for aid in the present crisis, and pledged them to bring me back. Small though I was, I was now in the hands of those still smaller. I had to face the wedding and even to thank God if my father-in-law were not in a rage and my lovely one grieved with me.

Permit me to pass over the ceremonies in silence; it is enough to say that we were married; yet though we were gay and lively as the days passed, there were, despite this, some lonely hours in which, being led to reflection, I encountered something I had never encountered before. What it was and how it came about you shall hear.

Everything around me conformed fully to my present shape and needs; the bottles and glasses were well-proportioned to a small drinker, indeed, much better on the whole than ours. To my small gums the delicate morsels had an unparalleled flavor, a kiss from my wife's dainty mouth was too enchanting for words, and I do not deny that novelty made all these associations highly pleasurable. Withal, I had unhappily not forgotten my previous state of existence. I felt within myself a measure of my former greatness, which made me unhappy and restless. Now, for the first time, I grasped what philosophers mean by their ideals, with which man is said to be so afflicted. I had an ideal of myself, and often in dreams I appeared to myself as a giant. In short, the wife, the ring, the dwarfed figure, and many other bonds made me so thoroughly and completely wretched that I began to give earnest thought to my deliverance.

As I was convinced that the whole magic lay in the ring, I determined to file it off. For this purpose I took several files from the court jeweler. Fortunately, I was left-handed and had never in my life done anything by rights. I held myself resolutely to my task; it was not slight: for the golden circlet, although it appeared so thin, had grown thicker in contracting from its former size. I gave all my leisure hours unobserved to this business, and when the metal was nearly filed through I was clever enough to step outside the door. This was well-advised; for all at once the golden circle sprang forcibly from my finger and my body shot up into the air with such vehemence that I really thought I had struck the sky, and in any case I should have broken through the dome of our summer palace, indeed, should have wrecked the entire pavilion with my brusque helplessness.

There I stood again, certainly much bigger, but also, it seemed to me, far more bewildered and ungainly. When I had recovered from my dizziness, I saw lying near me the casket, which felt rather heavy as I lifted it and trudged with it down the foot-path toward the post-tavern, where I immediately ordered horses and started travelling. On the way, I was not long in trying the pockets on either side. In place of the money, which seemed to have given out, I found a small key which fitted the casket, in which I found a fair compensation. As long as this lasted I used the carriage; afterwards I sold it in order to be able to go on by stage-coach. The casket was the last to be disposed of, for I kept on thinking it ought to fill itself once more. And so I came at last, though by a somewhat devious way, back to the hearth and the cook where first you came to know me.

Novelle

Novelle

THE heavy mist of an autumn morning veiled the spacious courts of the Prince's castle: but gradually, through the rising haze, the hunting party could more or less clearly be discerned, moving about on horseback and on foot. One could distinguish the busy activities of those near by: stirrups were lengthened or shortened, guns and ammunition were handed up, game bags were arranged, while the dogs, impatiently straining at their leashes, threatened to drag their handlers along with them. Here and there, too, a horse pranced, driven by its own fiery nature or excited by the spur of its rider, who, even in the half light of dawn, could not resist showing off. All were waiting for the Prince, who tarried too long in taking leave of his young wife.

Married only a short while before, they already knew the happiness of congenial dispositions; both were active and energetic, each liked to share the interests and pursuits of the other. The Prince's father had lived to see the time when it became common conviction that all members of the commonwealth should pass their days in equal industry, and, each in his own way, produce, earn, and enjoy.

How far this had been realized could be observed during these very days, when the main market was about to be held, an event which might almost be considered a fair. The day before, the Prince had led his wife on horseback through the busy display of wares, and had shown her how here the products of the mountain region and those of the plains were exchanged to mutual profit; with all this bustle before them he could demonstrate to her the industriousness of his people.

Although during these days the Prince talked almost exclusively with his advisers about such pressing matters, and worked especially closely with his Minister of Finance, yet his Huntmaster, too, would have his right: upon his pleading and in such favorable autumn weather the temptation to go on a long postponed hunt was irresistible. It would be a rare and special occasion for the household itself, as well as for the many strangers who had come to the fair.

The Princess reluctantly stayed at home; it had been planned to push far into the mountains in order to stir up the peaceable animals in those distant forests with an unexpected foray.

In parting, her husband suggested that she should go on a ride with Friedrich, the Prince's uncle. "I shall leave you our Honorio, too," he said, "as equerry and page. He will attend to everything." Saying this as he descended the stairs, he gave the necessary orders to a handsome youth, and soon thereafter left with guests and train.

The Princess, who had waved her handkerchief to her husband as long as he was still in the courtyard, now retired to those rooms at the back of the castle which commanded a free view towards the mountains, so much the lovelier as the castle itself stood on a height above the river, and on all sides afforded splendid and varied prospects. She found a fine telescope still in the position in which it had been left on the previous evening, when they had entertained themselves by looking across the rich hilly country to the height of the forest and the tall ruins of the ancient family castle, which stood out remarkably in the evening light. At that hour the great masses of light and shadow conveyed most vividly the grandeur of this impressive and venerable building. This morning, the sharp glass strikingly revealed the fall colors of those many kinds of trees which had struggled up between the stones, unhindered and undisturbed through many long years. But the Princess now tipped the telescope in the direction of a waste, stony plain, across which the hunting party could be expected to pass. She waited patiently for the moment when they were to come into view, and was not disappointed: for with the help of the powerfully magnifying instrument, her eyes could distinctly recognize the Prince and his chief equerry. Indeed, she waved once again with her handkerchief, as she noticed, or rather thought she noticed, that they halted for a moment and looked back toward the castle.

Friedrich, the Prince's uncle, was announced and came in, attended by an artist who carried a large portfolio under his arm. "Dear Cousin," said the vigorous old gentleman, "we have brought you some views of the old castle. They were sketched from various points and show how those strong battlements have, throughout many long years, resisted time and the elements; you will see how here and there the walls had to yield, and have crashed down in ruins. As a matter of fact, we only needed to make this wilderness accessible; it takes little more to surprise and delight any visitor."

As the old Prince commented upon the drawings he continued, "Here, as you advance along the narrow path through the outer ring to the fortress proper, one of the most massive rocks of the whole mountain rises before you. A tower has been built upon it, yet no one would be able to say where nature ends, and art and craftsmanship begin. Farther on you notice adjoining sidewalls, and dungeons, steeply terraced. But I am not quite accurate; this ancient summit is in reality almost completely surrounded by a forest. For one hundred and fifty years, no axe has sounded here, and everywhere huge trees have grown. Wherever you keep close to the walls, the trunks and roots of the smooth maple, the rough oak, and the slender pine will make it difficult for you to move. You must twist your way round them, and carefully plot your foot paths. See how well our artist has expressed the character of all this, with how much accuracy he has drawn the various kinds of trunks and roots, twisting among the masonry, and the huge boughs thrusting through the openings in the walls. It is a wilderness unlike any other, a unique place, where you can see traces of the long-vanished power of man in tenacious struggle with the ever-living, ever-working power of nature."

He put another sketch before her and continued: "What do you say to the castle yard? It has been made inaccessible by the collapse of the old gate tower, and had not been entered by anyone for countless years past. We tried to reach it from the side, and finally provided a convenient but hidden way by breaking through walls and blasting vaults. Once we were inside, there was no need for further clearing. Here you will notice a flat rock smoothed by nature; in some places enormous trees have found a chance to strike roots. They have grown slowly but vigorously, and now their branches reach up into the galleries on which the knights used to walk, indeed, even through doors and windows into the arched halls. We shall not drive them away—they have become the masters, and may remain so. Under deep piles of dried leaves we found the most extraordinary place, perfectly leveled, the like of which may perhaps not be found anywhere else in the world.

"Still, it is remarkable enough and must be seen at the very place itself, that on the steps leading up to the main tower a maple tree has taken root, and has grown so big that you can hardly get past it to ascend the highest tower from which you can enjoy an unlimited view. Yet up there, too, you are pleasantly in the shade: the same tree rises wonderfully high into the air and spreads over the whole area.

"Let us be grateful to this able artist who, in these sketches, conveys everything to us so admirably, as if we were actually on the spot. He has spent the best hours of the day and the season on them, and has for weeks actually lived there. In this corner we have set up a small but pleasant dwelling for him and the warden whom we assigned to him. You cannot believe, my dear, what a wonderful view into the country, the castle and the ruins he has created for himself there. But now, having sketched everything so neatly and tellingly, he will finish his drawings down here at his ease. We intend to decorate our garden hall with these pictures, and no one shall look at them so near to our civilized flower arrangements, arbors, and shady walks without wishing in contrast to contemplate up there all the evidence of the old and the new, the stubborn, inflexible and indestructible, but also the fresh, pliant and irresistible."

Honorio entered and announced that the horses were ready; the Princess turned to the uncle, "Why don't we ride up, and see in reality what you have shown me in these sketches. Ever since I have been here, I have heard about this project, and I am now all the more eager to see with my own eyes what seemed impossible in all accounts of it, and remains even now a little improbable in the pictures."

"Not yet, my dear," replied the Prince. "You saw in these pictures what eventually it can and will become; for the present many things are as yet only begun and a work of art requires completion if it is not to be put to shame by nature."

"Well then, let us at least ride towards it, if only to the lower parts. Today I feel like being where I can look far out into the world."

"As you will," replied the Prince.

"But let us go through the town," continued the lady, "across the great market place with its countless booths that have made it look like a little city, or an army camp. It is as if the wants and occupations of all the families in the land were there visibly spread out, focused in this one spot, and brought into the light of day. If you observe carefully, you can there see everything that man produces and needs. For a moment you imagine that money is not necessary, that all business could be conducted by barter, and of course, in a way, this is true enough. The Prince started me on this trend of thought last night, and now I have become doubly aware that here, where mountains and plain meet, both can clearly indicate their needs and their wishes. The highlander can process the timber of his forests in a thousand different shapes, and mold his iron for all kinds of uses, and the others from below come to meet him with a variety of products in which, often enough, you can hardly discover the original material or immediately recognize the purpose."

"I know," said the Prince, "that my nephew devotes much of his attention to these problems. What matters most at this season of the year is that more should be received than spent. To achieve this is, after all, the sum total of all national economy, as well as of the smallest household. Still, forgive me, my dear, I have never liked to ride through a market or fair: one is hindered and delayed at every step, and then the memory of that monstrous disaster always flares up in my mind. It burned itself, as it were, into my eyes. I was present on one occasion where just such a mass of wares was destroyed by flames. I had scarcely—"

"We must not waste these bright hours of daylight," interrupted the Princess, since the Prince had on several occasions frightened her with a minute description of the catastrophe. On one of his journeys, he had gone to bed in the best inn on the market place, which was just then swarming with the noise and bustle of a fair. He had been exceedingly tired, and suddenly in the dead of the night, was awakened by screams, and by flames billowing towards his lodging.

The Princess hastened to mount her favorite horse, and led her half-reluctant, half-eager companion, not up the mountain through the rear gate, but by the front gate down the hill. For who would not have enjoyed riding at her side and following her wherever she led? Even Honorio had willingly forgone the very pleasure of a hunt in order to devote himself to her.

160

As might have been anticipated, they could ride across the market place only step by step. But with her singular charm the Princess made any delay entertaining by her spirited comments. "I seem to be repeating yesterday's lesson," she said, "since we are by necessity held up." The crowd pressed so closely around them that they could continue only at the slowest pace. The people liked to see the young princess, and by their pleased smiles indicated their satisfaction that the first lady of the land should also be the loveliest and the most graceful.

It was a motley crowd: mountain people, who lived quietly among their rocks, firs, and spruces, lowlanders from the hills, plains and fields, and small-town tradesmen—all were assembled here. The Princess looked at the people for a while, then turned to her companions, and told them how she was struck by the fact that wherever they came from, these country people used far more material for their clothes than necessary, more cloth and linen, more ribbons for trimming. "It really seems as if the women could not be bedecked enough and the men not puffed out enough to please themselves."

"Let us allow them that," replied the uncle. "Spend their extra money where they will, the people are happy doing it, and happiest when they spend it on dressing up." The Princess nodded in agreement.

They had finally reached an open space which led to the outskirts of the town. There at the end of the line of booths and stalls they noticed a fairly large wooden structure. from which there suddenly came an earsplitting roar. It was the feeding time of the wild animals which were exhibited there. They could hear the fierce voice of the lion which was perhaps more appropriate to the forest and desert; the horses shuddered and neighed, and everybody felt the terrible force with which the king of the wilderness drew attention to himself amid the innocent pursuits of a civilized community. They approached the building and saw huge, garish posters representing those exotic animals in the crudest and most violent colors. In these pictures, by which the peaceful citizen was to be irresistibly tempted, a tremendous, fierce tiger attacked a Negro, and was about to tear him to pieces; a lion stood in solemn majesty, as if he could find no prey worthy of him; and compared to these two powerful animals, the others, equally striking and uncommon, attracted less attention.

"Let us stop here on our trip back," said the Princess, "and look at these rare creatures." "It is a strange thing," replied the Prince, "that people want forever to be excited by something terrible. Inside the tent, I am sure, the tiger lies perfectly calm, but here it has to pounce wildly upon a Negro, so that we should believe that the same thing may be seen inside. Is there not enough murder and violent death in the world, enough burning and destruction? Must the ballad singers repeat it at every corner? People want to be frightened, so that they may afterwards feel all the more vividly, how pleasant and delightful it is to breathe freely."

But no matter how many anxious thoughts these fearful pictures produced in their minds, all were swept aside as the group passed through the gate and reached a most cheerful scene. The river, along which they rode, was narrow here, and could take only light boats, but, by the same name, it was eventually to enrich the life of faraway lands. The group moved on through well-tended fruit and pleasure gardens, coming gradually into the open and more thickly settled countryside. They passed through an occasional thicket or small wood and were delighted by a view here and there of charming villages. Soon they entered a sloping valley, its grass recently mowed for the second time, smooth as velvet, watered by a stream that rushed towards them from a spring higher up. The woods were left behind and after a steep climb they reached a higher and even more open spot. Some distance ahead, beyond clumps of trees, rose like wooded peaks the old castle, the goal of their journey. One could not reach the place without occasionally turning around, and behind them to the left, they saw through a clearing, the Prince's castle bathed in the light of the morning sun. The upper part of the town lay half hidden in a light mist of smoke, and down farther to the right, they recognized the lower town and a few bends of the river with its meadows and mills. On the other side there extended a wide and fertile stretch of land.

Having satisfied themselves with so magnificent a view, or rather, as often happens when we look out from a high place, doubly eager to find an even wider view, they rode along a broad, stony stretch until they saw before them the green crowned summit of the castle ruins, a few old trees at its foot. They passed through these, and soon found themselves at the steepest, least accessible side. Giant rocks lay there untouched by change since the beginning of time, solid, towering high. What had fallen among them was irregularly piled up in huge slabs and broken pieces—as if to bar even the boldest from any attempt to scale it. But the sheerest and most precipitous incline seems to challenge youth, and to try to master and conquer is for them the greatest delight. The Princess was ready to make an attempt, Honorio was at hand, and the Prince, a little more concerned with comfort, but unwilling to appear timid, joined in. The horses were left there under the trees, and the party hoped to reach the point where an enormous projecting rock offered a level place from which they would have a view not only as vast as that of a bird's eye, but at the same time most picturesque.

The sun, nearly at its height, lent its clearest light; the Prince's residence with all its ramified buildings, wings, cupolas and towers stood out magnificently. The upper town spread before them, even the lower could now easily be seen; indeed, through the telescope they could distinguish the individual booths on the market square. Honorio was in the habit of always carrying this useful instrument on his rides. You could look up and down the river and follow on one side the terraced land and on the other the slowly rising, rolling, and fertile slopes. There were innumerable villages— as a matter of fact, it had long been a subject of contention, how many one might be able to count from up here.

A serene stillness lay over the wide expanse—as it so often is at noon when, as the ancients said, Pan is asleep and all nature holds her breath, lest he be awakened.

"It is not the first time," said the Princess, "that standing on such a high and commanding spot, I realize how simple and peaceful nature can look, and how it gives you the impression that the world is without conflict; but when you return to the dwellings of men, whether they be rich or poor, comfortable or cramped, there is always something to fight or quarrel about, to settle or to straighten out."

Honorio, who had meanwhile looked through his telescope towards the town, suddenly called out, "Look, look, there is a fire in the market place!" They could see a little smoke, but the daylight dimmed the brightness of the flames. "The fire is spreading!" cried Honorio, still looking through the instrument. The Princess could now see the conflagration with the naked eye. From time to time a red flame shot up, and smoke rose.

"Let us get back," said the Prince. "I don't like this; I have always been afraid of having to go through such a disaster again."

When they had reached the foot of the castle where the horses had been left, the Princess said to the old Prince, "You ride ahead, quickly, and take the groom along; leave Honorio with me, we will follow." The uncle accepted this reasonable and prudent suggestion, and rode, as fast as the ground permitted, down the rough, stony slope.

When the Princess mounted her horse, Honorio said, "Do ride slowly, Your Highness, all fire equipment in the town and in the castle is in the best order; not even such an extraordinary and unexpected emergency will cause confusion. But here where we are, the ground is bad, there are small stones and stubbly grass, and it is not safe to ride too fast; anyhow, by the time we reach the town, the fire will be extinguished." The Princess did not quite believe that; she saw the smoke spreading and even thought she had noticed a shooting flame and heard an explosion. She remembered all the terrifying pictures which her uncle's repeated story of the fire that he had once witnessed had so vividly impressed upon her.

That catastrophe, in its striking suddenness, had been frightful enough to leave behind it for life a horror of its recurrence. At night a furious fire had seized booth after booth on the wide and crowded market square, long before the people sleeping in and near these buildings could have been shaken out of their deep dreams. The old Prince, a stranger in the town, had just fallen asleep after a weary journey. He had leapt to the window and seen everything fearfully illuminated; flames darting in all directions, from right and left, rolled towards him. The houses on the square, reddened by the reflection, seemed to glow, about to burst into flames at any moment. Below him the fire raged relentlessly; boards cracked, beams crackled, canvas flew up and the dusky, tattered burning ends wafted about in the air as if evil spirits in their own element, forever changing shape, were engaged in a wild dance, consuming themselves, only here and there emerging from the glowing heat. Everybody screamed and howled, and tried to save what lay nearest; servants and their masters made every effort to drag away bales that the fire had already seized, and to tear away from the burning scaffolding this or that in order to throw into boxes what they would in the end have to leave to the flames. How many of them worked for only a moment's respite from the crackling fire, and as they looked about for a chance of a breathing spell, all their belongings were swallowed by the flames. What lay still in darkness on one side was smoldering

on the other. A few determined, stubborn people grimly resisted the enemy and managed to save some of their belongings, though at a loss of eyebrows and hair. All these scenes
of mad confusion now rose again before the Princess's mind;
the clear view of the morning was overclouded, her eyes
darkened; wood and field had assumed a look of strangeness
and anguish.

As they entered the peaceful valley, hardly aware of its refreshing coolness, they had gone only a few paces beyond
the source of the brook when the Princess noticed far down
in the thicket something strange. She recognized it immediately as the tiger, coming towards them as she had seen him
in the poster only a short time ago. This sight, together with
the picture that had just been in her mind, gave her the
strangest feeling. "Get away! Princess!" cried Honorio, "get
away!" She turned her horse towards the steep hill from
which they had just come. The young man drew his pistol
and, approaching the animal, fired when he seemed near
enough. But he missed, the tiger sprang to the side, the horse
was startled, and the provoked beast pursued his course
straight towards the Princess. She rode as fast as her horse
would go, up the steep, rocky slope, forgetting for a moment
that so delicate a creature, unused to such exertion, might
not be able to stand it for long. Driven on by the Princess in
her terror, it did overexert itself, stumbling again and again
on the loose gravel, and finally fell exhausted to the ground
after one last violent effort. The lady, resolute and skillful,
was instantly on her feet; the horse, too, rose. The tiger came
nearer, though not rapidly—the uneven ground, the sharp
stones, seemed to hinder his progress. Honorio rode immediately behind him, and slowed down as he was beside the
beast. This seemed to give him new strength and, at the
same moment, both reached the place where the Princess
stood by her horse. Honorio bent down and with his second
pistol shot the animal through the head. It fell, and as it lay

stretched out in full length it seemed to reveal the might and terror of which now only the physical form was left. Honorio had leapt from his horse and knelt on the tiger, restraining its last movements and holding his drawn hunting knife in his hand. He was a handsome sight as he sprang forward, very much as the Princess had seen him before in ring and lance tournaments. Just so in the riding course would his bullet, as he darted by, hit the brow of the Turk's-head on the pole, right under the turban. Just so, elegantly prancing up, would he pick the Moor's-head off the ground with his naked saber. He was dexterous and lucky in all such arts, and this now stood him in good stead.

"Do kill him." said the Princess. "I am afraid he will hurt you with his claws."

"No," replied the young man, "he is dead enough and I do not want to spoil this skin which next winter shall shine on your sleigh."

"Don't speak lightly. A moment like this calls forth our most solemn feelings."

"I was never more solemn in my life," said Honorio. "But for that very reason, I think only of what is most joyful—I look at this tiger's skin as it accompanies you in your pleasures."

"It would always remind me of this terrible moment," she replied.

"Still, it is a less pretentious sign of triumph," replied the young man, "than when the weapons of slain enemies are displayed in proud procession before the victor."

"I shall always remember your courage and skill when I see it." replied the Princess, "and I need not add that as long as you live, you can depend on my gratitude and the Prince's favor. But rise, the animal is dead, let us see what should be done next. Do rise now." "Since I am already kneeling before you," replied Honorio, "which I know I dare not do under any other circumstance, let me beg you to assure me at this moment of your favor, and grace. I have often asked the

Prince for permission to travel. Surely he who is fortunate enough to sit at your table, whom you honor with the privilege of entertaining your company, should have seen something of the world. Travelers come to us from all parts, and when the conversation turns to some city, some important place anywhere in the world, the question is certain to be asked of us whether we have been there. None are credited with any wisdom except those who have seen it all; it is almost as if we had to inform ourselves mainly for the benefit of others."

"Do rise," insisted the Princess, "I should not like to ask a favor or make a request of my husband which I know would go against his convictions; but I am sure that it would be easy to dispel the one reason why he has so far kept you here. He wanted to see you develop into an independent, self-reliant nobleman, to do yourself and him credit abroad, as you have done hitherto at court. I should think that to-day's courageous act will be as good a recommendation as any young man could hope to have for his travels."

The Princess did not have time to notice that sadness, rather than pleasure, crossed his face. Nor did Honorio have an opportunity to express his feelings, for a woman with a boy at her hand came running up the hill in great haste, straight towards the two. Honorio collected himself and rose. The woman, crying loudly, threw herself on the body of the tiger. This action, as well as her gaudy and strange, yet neat, costume, left no doubt that she was the owner and keeper of the animal. The boy had dark eyes and jet black hair, and held a flute in his hand. He knelt next to his mother, deeply moved and, like her, cried, though a little less violently.

The woman's furious outbursts were followed by a sputtering flood of words, like a stream leaping in gushes from one rock to the next. She used a sort of natural language, brief and abrupt, yet at the same time compelling and pathetic. It would be impossible to translate it into our kind of speech;

its general meaning was this: "They have murdered you, poor creature, murdered you needlessly! You were tame and would certainly have lain down to wait for us. Your feet were tender and your claws had lost their power. You missed the hot sun that would have given them strength. You were the most beautiful among your kind; whoever saw such a regal tiger magnificently stretched out in sleep as you now lie here, dead, never to rise again! When you awoke early in the morning and opened your jaws and showed your red tongue, it almost seemed as if you were smiling. And even though you roared, you still took your feed—almost playfully —from the hands of a woman, from the fingers of a child. For how long now have we accompanied you on your journeys, how long has your company meant everything to us. In truth, for us, out of the eater came forth meat, and out of the strong came forth sweetness. It will be so no more! Woe! Woe!"

She had not finished her lamentations, when a group of riders came galloping along the side of the castle mountain. They were soon recognized as the Prince's hunting party, he himself at their head. They had pursued their game in the hills beyond, and had noticed the clouds of smoke. Racing across valleys and ravines as if in fierce chase, they had taken the most direct way towards that awful sign. As they rode along the rocky slope, they stopped short and seemed startled by the unexpected sight of the group which stood out prominently in the wide empty space. After the first moments of recognition and silence, they recovered their presence of mind and what was not obvious was explained in a few words. There stood the Prince, contemplating this strange and unheard of incident, about him a circle of riders and those who had followed him hurriedly on foot. It was clear what had to be done next and the Prince was busy giving the necessary orders when suddenly a man forced his way into the circle. He was tall, and dressed in the same curiously gaudy manner as the woman and the child. The whole family now joined in sorrow and dismay. The man composed himself and, standing at a respectful distance from the Prince, said, "This is no time for lamentation. My Lord, the lion, too, is loose; he is coming this way towards the mountains; but, pray, spare him, have mercy, so that he may not die like this poor beast."

"The lion?" asked the Prince, "have you found his track?"

"Yes, sir! One of the peasants down there who had quite needlessly taken refuge in a tree directed me up this way, a little farther to the left. But I saw this crowd of people and horses, and came here to get more information and perhaps help."

"Very well, then," ordered the Prince, "let the hunting party move up in this direction. Load your guns and proceed cautiously; it does not matter if you drive him into the deep woods. But I am afraid that in the end we may not be able to spare your lion. Why were you careless enough to let the animals escape?"

"When the fire broke out," replied the man, "we remained quiet and watchful; it spread fast, but at some distance from us; we had water enough to protect ourselves, but a sudden explosion threw the fire in our direction, indeed, beyond us. We were suddenly too rushed, and now we are ruined."

The Prince was still busy, giving orders; but for a moment everything seemed to halt: a man came running down from the old castle—it was the warden who was in charge of the artist's workshop, and who lived there and supervised the workmen. He was out of breath, but managed to tell briefly that the lion was lying perfectly quiet in the sun behind the upper ring-wall, at the foot of a century-old beech tree. He seemed almost annoyed as he concluded—"Why did I take my gun into town yesterday to have it cleaned? If I had had it with me, he would never have got up again. His skin would have belonged to me, and I would have boasted about it all my life, and rightly, too."

The Prince, whose military experience stood him in good stead and who was used to finding himself in a situation where unavoidable danger threatened from several sides, said to the man, "What guarantee can you give me that if we spare your lion, he might not cause a good deal of harm among the people?"

"This woman and child," answered the father hastily, "are willing to keep him tame and quiet until I can bring up a cage, and we can carry him back harmless and unharmed."

At that moment the boy put his flute to his lips—an instrument that used to be called the soft or sweet flute. It was short-stemmed like a pipe, and anyone who played it well could produce the most delicious tones. Meanwhile the Prince inquired of the warden how the lion had come up. "By the hollow way, which is walled in on both sides and which has always been and will always be the only real road of access. Two footpaths that used to lead up have been so blocked up that there is now only that one way by which one can reach the magic castle which the place is to become through Prince Friedrich's taste and talent."

After some reflection, while looking at the child who had continued to play softly as if preluding, the Prince turned to Honorio and said, "You have done much today; now complete the day's work. Guard that narrow road; keep your rifles ready, but do not shoot until the animal cannot be driven back in any other way. If necessary, make a fire which will frighten him if he should want to come down. The man and woman must be responsible for the rest." Honorio hurried to execute these orders.

The child continued to play, not really a tune, but an irregular sequence of tones, and, possibly for that reason, it was especially moving. Everyone seemed enchanted by these melodious passages, when the father began to speak in a curiously dignified and exalted manner.

"God has given wisdom to the Prince and also the

knowledge to recognize that all God's works are wise, each in its own way. Behold the rock, standing fast and motionless, defying the weather and the sunshine. Primeval trees crown its summit, and thus enhanced, it commands a wide view; but if any part of it should fall, it would not remain what it was: it will crumble in many pieces and cover the slope of the mountain. But they will not stay there, either; they will tumble on down, the brook will receive them and carry them to the river. They cannot resist, they are no longer stubborn and rough; smooth and rounded they travel even faster from river to river, and on to the ocean where the hosts of giants march, and dwarfs abound in the depths.

"But who shall praise the glory of the Lord, Whom the stars praise through all Eternity? Why look afar? Behold the bee, how it gathers busily late in the fall, building its house true and level, architect and workman at once. See the ant, it knows its way and loses it not. It builds its dwelling of grass and earth and pine needles. It piles it high and arches it in; but its work has been in vain—the horse stamps and scrapes it to pieces; look, he has trodden down those delicate beams and scattered the planks, impatiently he snorts and cannot rest; for the Lord has made the horse the comrade of the wind and the companion of the storm, that he may carry man where he wills, and woman where she desires. But in the forest of palms there appeared the lion; proudly he roams the desert ruling over all animals and nothing will resist him. Yet man knows how to tame him, and the fiercest of living creatures has reverence for the image of God, in which, too, the angels are made, who serve the Lord and His servants. For in the den of lions Daniel was not afraid; he remained steadfast and faithful and the wild roaring did not interrupt his song of praise."

These words were spoken with a kind of natural enthusiasm and accompanied here and there by the child's sweet music. When the father had ended, the boy began to sing with much skill in a clear, melodious voice. The father in turn took the flute and accompanied the child as he sang:

> From the dens, I, in a deeper,
> Prophet's song of praise can hear;
> Angel-host he hath for keeper,
> Needs the good man there to fear?

> Lion, lioness, agazing,
> Mildly pressing round him came;
> Yea, that humble, holy praising,
> It hath made them tame.

The father continued playing the flute, while the mother occasionally joined in as second voice.

The effect was especially striking when the child began to rearrange the lines of the song in a different sequence and thereby produced, not a new meaning but a far greater intensity of feeling.

> Angel-host around doth hover,
> Us in heavenly tones to cheer;
> In the dens our head doth cover,—
> Needs the poor child there to fear?

> For that humble, holy praising
> Will permit no evil nigh:
> Angels hover, watching, gazing,
> Who so safe as I?

All three now joined with force and conviction.

> For th' Eternal rules above us,
> Lands and oceans rules His will;
> Lions even as lambs shall love us,
> And the proudest waves be still.

Whetted sword to scabbard cleaving,
Faith and Hope victorious see:
Strong, who, loving and believing,
Prays, O Lord, to Thee.

The others were silent and listened intently. Only when the music ceased could one observe the impression it had made. They all seemed calmed and everyone was moved in his own way. The Prince, as if only now fully aware of the danger that had threatened earlier, looked at his wife who, holding his arm, covered her eyes with an embroidered handkerchief. She was relieved that the oppressive feeling with which her heart had been filled only a few minutes before had now gone from her. Complete silence reigned over the crowd—they appeared to have forgotten the terror of the fire below and of the lion above them who might arise at any moment.

The Prince stirred the group with a sign to bring the horses. He turned to the woman and said, "Do you really think that you can calm the lion when you find him, by your song, the singing of this child, and the music of this flute? And that you can take him back to his cage, harmless and uninjured?" They assured him that this was so. The warden was given to them as a guide. The Prince and a few of his attendants left hurriedly while the Princess, accompanied by the rest, followed more leisurely. Mother and son and the warden, who had meanwhile armed himself with a rifle, proceeded to climb towards the mountain.

Before they entered the narrow roadway which gave them access to the castle they found the hunters busy heaping up dry brushwood to light a fire if it were required. "There is no need for that," said the woman. "All will go well and peaceably."

Farther on, sitting on a part of the wall, they found Honorio on guard, his double-barreled rifle in his lap, as if prepared for any eventuality. He seemed hardly to notice the approaching group, but sat, lost in deep thought, looking about absently. The woman asked him not to allow the fire to be lit, but Honorio appeared not to pay any attention to her words. She spoke again, more urgently, and said: "Young man, you have slain my tiger—but I do not bear you any ill will. Now spare my lion and I will bless you."

Honorio looked straight ahead at the setting sun. "You are looking towards evening," continued the woman, "and you are right—there is much to do there. Hurry, do not delay, you will conquer. But first of all conquer yourself!" At this he seemed to smile; the woman went on her way and only turned once more to look back on him. The sun cast a glowing light over his face—she thought that she had never seen a more beautiful youth.

"If your child," said the warden, "can, as you are convinced, with his flute and his singing, entice the lion and pacify him, we shall get hold of him very easily. He lies close to the broken walls through which we have had to make a passageway into the castle yard since the main gate is blocked by rubble. When the child leads him inside, I can close the opening without much trouble. And at the right moment the boy can slip away by one of the small winding staircases in the corner. We must hide, but I shall place myself so that I can have a bullet ready if the child should need help."

"All these precautions are unnecessary; God and our own skill, our faith and fortune are our best aid." "That may be," replied the warden, "but I know my duties. Let me lead you first by a rather difficult path to the top of the wall, immediately opposite the opening I have mentioned. Let the lad then descend into the arena and lead away the animal if it will follow him." This was done. Warden and mother saw from their hiding place above how the child descended the winding stairs, showed himself in the open space of the courtyard and disappeared again in the dark opening on the other side. They could hear the tone of his flute, which gradually grew fainter, and at last, ceased altogether. The pause was ominous enough; the old hunter, accustomed to every kind of peril, felt the oppressive suspense in this extraordinary incident. He would have preferred to engage the dangerous beast himself. But the mother, cheerful and assured, and bending over to listen, did not betray the slightest apprehension.

At last the flute could be heard again, the child, his eyes bright and pleased, emerged from the dark cavern, and behind him the lion, walking slowly and, as it seemed, with some difficulty. Now and then the animal tried to lie down, but the boy led him in a half circle through the autumn-tinged trees. Eventually, in the last rays of the sun pouring in through a break in the ruined walls, he sat down as if transfigured. Once again he began his soothing song which we cannot refrain from repeating:

> From the dens, I, in a deeper,
> Prophet's song of praise can hear;
> Angel-host he hath for keeper,
> Needs the good man there to fear?

> Lion, lioness, agazing,
> Mildly pressing round him came;
> Yea, that humble, holy praising,
> It hath made them tame.

Meanwhile the lion had lain down close to the child and lifted his heavy right paw into his lap. The boy, as he sang, stroked it and soon noticed that a sharp thorn had caught between the balls of the animal's foot. He carefully extracted it, and with a smile took the silken handkerchief from his neck to bind up the forbidding foot of the huge beast. His mother was overjoyed and, bending back with her arms out-

176

stretched, would have shouted and clapped applause as she was accustomed had not a rough grip of the warden reminded her that the danger was not yet over.

The child sang on triumphantly, having first introduced the tune with a few notes on the flute.

> For th' Eternal rules above us,
> Lands and oceans rules His will;
> Lions even as lambs shall love us,
> And the proudest waves be still.
>
> Whetted sword to scabbard cleaving,
> Faith and Hope victorious see:
> Strong, who, loving and believing,
> Prays, O Lord, to Thee.

If it is possible to imagine that the features of so fierce a monster, the tyrant of the forest and the despot of the animal kingdom, could display an expression of friendliness, of grateful contentment, it might have been witnessed on this occasion. The child, with his exalted look, seemed now like a mighty victorious conqueror. The lion, on the other hand, was not so much vanquished—for his strength though concealed was still in him—as tamed and surrendered to his own peaceful will. The child fluted and sang on, transposing the lines in his fashion and adding to them.

> And so to good children bringeth
> Blessed Angel help in need;
> Fetters o'er the cruel flingeth,
> Worthy act with wings doth speed.
>
> So have tamed, and firmly iron'd
> To a poor child's feeble knee,
> Him, the forest's lordly tyrant,
> Pious Thought and Melody.

177

Rinehart Editions